S0-DYT-819

PRIVATE
RESERVE
A DOSSIER NOVELLA

PRIVATE
RESERVE
A DOSSIER NOVELLA

CATHRYN FOX

This book is a work of fiction. Names, characters, places, and incidents are the product of the author's imagination or are used fictitiously. Any resemblance to actual events, locales, or persons, living or dead, is coincidental.

Copyright © 2017 by Cathryn Fox. All rights reserved, including the right to reproduce, distribute, or transmit in any form or by any means. For information regarding subsidiary rights, please contact the Publisher.

Entangled Publishing, LLC
10940 S Parker Rd
Suite 327
Parker, CO 80134
rights@entangledpublishing.com

Scorched is an imprint of Entangled Publishing, LLC.

Edited by Candace Havens
Cover design by LJ Anderson
Cover art by OGphoto/Getty Images

Manufactured in the United States of America

First Edition March 2017

entangled
scorched

To Joanna D, for being such a great friend and inspiration.

Chapter One

Why, again, am I doing this?

Oh right, because of that long-ago stupid New Years Eve party where I, along with a group of my best friends, decided to celebrate the second half of our twenties in an epic way.

Just how epic, you ask?

Oh, let's just say we're to go on an adventure and not come home until we've had legendary sex—delicious, salacious, rough and dirty, "bang me against the wall and leave me bruised" sex. Well, that's the kind I want anyway. But sadly, I see no glimmer of anything quite so wicked in my dull future.

That fateful night two years ago, our friend Harper, the most adventurous and imaginative of us, decided we should all put our names in a hat then draw one out, keeping it a secret. On the month of your twenty-fifth birthday, whoever pulled your name would send you a dossier detailing an entire destination adventure designed specifically for you.

A half a bottle of champagne later—okay, three-quarters

of a bottle and four Jell-O shots—putting my name in a hat for a sexy endeavor seemed like a good idea, a fun thing to do. Then again, so did all those shots of Patron. Until I woke up half dead with a damn headache, bloodshot eyes, and my bed as cold as the liquor I'd consumed.

Why is it I feel like I'm going to wake up the same way after this journey?

"You okay back there?" the cabbie asks in a thick Italian accent.

Shit, when had the vehicle stopped? "Yeah, thanks." I look at the meter, do a quick mental conversion, and hand over a hundred euros. Tote bag and purse in hand, I open the door and breathe in the fragrant county air as I exit.

On a white wooden swing at the side of the sprawling Tuscan villa that looks like a castle, an elderly couple sips wine and waves to me as I fully commit to this adventure. Go me! Near them, another older couple slowly walks the shrub-lined path toward what looks to be a wine tasting area. I scan the bar and see nothing but a sea of silver hair. Dammit, the place looks more like a retirement home than a hot spot for a hook-up.

I turn when my driver pulls my suitcase from the trunk and sets it beside my Jimmy Choos. The shoes are a secret indulgence, one I can't really afford on the salary of the entry-level marketing job where I seem to be stuck, thanks to the boys' club mentality at Resolve Solutions. What a way to put my hard earned business degree to use. When I get home, I seriously have to start looking for something else, despite my affection for a steady paycheck, no matter how small it is. A disgruntled groan rises in my throat. Like finding another marketing job in an overcrowded workforce is such an easy task.

Late summer sunshine spills over me as the cabbie slides into the front seat and drives away. Dust kicks up behind the vehicle, and I push those depressing thoughts out of my head for the time being, choosing instead to admire the gorgeous vineyard estate sprawled before me — calm, tranquil, historic… absolutely breathtaking.

So why, again, am I here for a three-week countryside getaway — in a place clearly populated with geriatrics — when the girl sponsoring my trip could have sent me to a London strip joint with hot, naked, *young* men? *Le sigh.* My older brother Sean often goes to London on business, and from some of his stories, I so want to go someday.

Maybe I'll send Kennedy to a club next month when I prepare her dossier. I'd been saving for months now, determined to give her something spectacular. I don't care if she's shy and introverted. At least one of us girls should have a hot guy gyrating on her at some point in her life, right? I'm sure, in the end, she'll thank me for it.

My sponsor, however… I'm 100 percent certain I won't be thanking her for anything. Seriously, though, did she expect me to hook up with some grandpa? I'll be twenty-five this month, not ninety. Clearly, I need a new friend, one who knows me and understands what I want.

You never tell anyone what you want.

Yeah, yeah, whatever.

I exhale an exaggerated breath, pick up my suitcase and make my way along the path leading to the hotel. I shade my eyes from the afternoon sun and look off into the distance, my heels clicking on the walkway as I take in the rows of grapes lining the hillside. A sweet, citrusy smell reaches my nose, and I breathe it in. Then I nearly jump out of my heels when a cannon sounds off, not too far from where I'm standing. What the hell! A frightened flock of birds takes flight, and understanding dawns. The noise protects the fruit from unwanted inhabitants. Good. The more grapes for the vintner, the more wine for me. Since it's highly unlikely I'll be able to have the kind of sex I crave while on a trip that can only be described as a snooze fest, at least there'll be plenty to drink.

From the corner of my eye I catch movement and angle my head to see a hot guy with longish hair, dressed in ripped jeans and a snug T-shirt, walking around the side of the building. A hot *young* guy. Well then, perhaps I'd been too judgy of the place. Mr. Hottie is looking around, glancing over his shoulder, and scoping out the vineyard like he's up to no good.

Interesting. If I weren't so damn exhausted, I'd follow him, but four hundred hours of flying has pretty much done me in. That doesn't mean after a good night's sleep I won't seek him out, see what kind of trouble he's up to—see what kind we can get in together.

Damned if this trip isn't starting to look up.

Feeling a little happier with this whole set up, I step into the warm lobby of the main castle, now converted to a hotel. The sun beams in the windows, heating the place up to a bazillion degrees. I take note of the elderly gentleman with gray hair behind the check-in counter. I'm kind of tired after the long flight from Seattle, so I'm really hoping my room is ready. Then again, it's not like the place is bustling. I spin around and catalog the empty lobby. When I turn back to the man behind the counter and meet Mediterranean-blue eyes, my heart gives a little jolt, and I can't help but think of *him*.

The guy I still love.

The guy I never, ever want to see again.

The guy I'd do anything to see again.

I shake my head to clear my thoughts.

Nope, not thinking about my ex—ever again.

"Olivia Fraser," I say, stepping up to the smiling man behind the counter.

"Welcome. We've been expecting you." The man pulls a sheet of paper from a manila folder, and an arthritic hand slides it across the countertop to me. "Please fill in your information and sign in here."

I do as he asks, and he hands me a key. Not the electronic kind used in the states. No, this metal key is vintage, and as big as my hand. While I love modern amenities, like air conditioning, I kind of dig the rustic charm of the key. Despite all my complaining, the place does hold a certain appeal. If they kept it old school and added a few modern touches, they might be able to draw a younger crowd. I smile as I envision the changes I'd make to appeal to my generation, then shake my head. If only Revolve Solutions would give me a chance to prove myself, let me show them what I can do.

"We put you in the private cottage at the base of Abrusco."

"Abrusco?"

His smile is gentle and warm as he waves toward the window showcasing his beautiful countryside. "There are many different grapes grown here, and your accommodation is at the base of where the Abrusco variety are grown. They're coming on ripe, so feel free to taste a few before they're harvested." The man comes around the counter to help me with my bag, but I hold my hand up to stop him.

"I got it," I say, partly because I'm an independent woman, and partly because the guy is fifty years past retirement age.

He nods and hands me a map of the vineyard and buildings, and points to the location of my room. I head back outside and hoof it to the other side of the villa, my over packed bag difficult to maneuver on the old cobblestone walkways. A yawn pulls at me when I finally make it to my cottage, and I jiggle the key into the lock and step into the room. First impression: nice, clean, simple. My gaze moves over the dresser, dinette table, kitchenette, and small bathroom on the main level, then slides up to take in the double bed in the upstairs loft, along with a balcony. I snort. With my luck, I'll probably drink too much wine and end up falling down the damn stairs and breaking my neck on the way to the bathroom.

I drop my luggage, drag my tired ass up the five steps,

and peel open the curtains to reveal a spectacular view of the vineyards. It really is remarkable. I crack the door and breathe in the fresh country air, but I go still when I hear two male voices below my window. Gruff. Angry. Incensed. My body tightens. Are they fighting? Nosey girl that I am, I push the door open a bit more and quietly step out, but what I see has my breath catching and heat exploding inside me.

No. Frigging. Way.

As the two men grab at each other—their hands tugging, groping; their lips crashing, devouring—I stand there immobilized, unable to move, breathe, or think with any sort of clarity.

Oh. My. God. This has to be the hottest, sexiest thing I've ever seen.

Knees locked, I stare, mesmerized by the way they clutch at each other. So needy. So damn hungry. I recognize Mr. Hottie from earlier, but the other guy has on a hat that masks his features. It's emblazed with the Italian flag, and Gil Azzurri, which represents the national soccer federation. I only know that because my ex was a fan, and I'd watched a few games with him years ago.

The hat's bill covers the man's face, and his voice is so deep and gruff with arousal it's hard to make out what he's saying. But the way he's gripping his lover's hair, angling his head for a deeper kiss as he thrusts his tongue inside, is the hottest freaking thing I've ever witnessed. Holy hell, the way they want each other, grabbing and tugging to get closer, the raw neediness of it all, just about has me orgasming. I grip the metal rail as heat charges to my sex, my nipples puckering so hard they poke through my lace bra, demanding attention.

Blue Hat breaks the kiss. "Down on your knees," he demands, shoving hard on Mr. Hottie's shoulder. The man sinks to his knees obediently, his face inches from the guy's bulging crotch.

My entire body breaks out in a sweat, and I quiver from the top of my head to the tips of my toes. I sip air quietly, my heart crashing, my eyelids fluttering, unable to believe what I've stumbled upon. What I'm doing is wrong and I should go inside to give them the privacy they deserve, and are clearly seeking, but I can't seem to tear my gaze away. Who knew I was such a voyeur?

Blue Hat rips into his jeans, popping the button and drawing the zipper down. The sound cuts through the quiet of the mountainside, but I'm breathing so hard by this point I'm worried they're going to hear me. As I squeeze my legs, my swollen clit rubs against my panties and I want to touch myself, to get off as I watch them get each other off.

Blue Hat grips the other man's chin. "Open that pretty mouth of yours," he commands. His hat tilts, angles to the side like he's questioning something. "You do want to suck my cock, don't you?"

Dimples flash on Mr. Hottie's face. "Yes," he murmurs, then he widens his mouth, inviting his friend in.

"That's so fucking nice," Blue Hat says, brushing his thumb over the man's bottom lip. "Tell you what. You suck me real good, show me how much you want my cock, and then maybe I'll bend you over and fuck you like those brown eyes are begging me to."

Mr. Hottie groans as Blue Hat shackles one of his wrists and brings his hand to his cock. He keeps his hand locked on the guy's arm and follows the motion as he jerks him off. Precum glistens on his crown, and Mr. Hottie leans in, licking the salty treat from the man's gorgeous, bulbous head, sliding his tongue along the slit to get every last drop. Blue Hat growls and jerks forward, shoving his cock to the back of Mr. Hottie's throat. The guy chokes. No freaking wonder.

"Open your throat. Take it deeper," he orders, his hands fisting in the man's hair, and urging him on. "Yeah, that's it.

Show me how much you want me to fuck that sweet hole of yours."

My sex is throbbing, my clit demanding attention. Unable to help myself, I slip my hand into my jeans, and touch myself. I bite my bottom lip to stifle a cry of pleasure. Never having been so turned on in my life, I rub furiously, and my muscles clench. Dammit, I need to slow down, or I'm going to shatter into a million pieces, and I'm just not ready for this to be over. I use a softer touch, wanting to draw out every second, and rock my hips in much the same manner as Blue Hat.

"Look at you. Such a greedy bastard. Taking me so deep because you want your ass fucked."

I whimper then clamp my hand over my mouth. Shit. I feel a quick flash of panic, but the two guys are so lost in each other, they don't hear me. Thank God. If they stop now, I might just die.

Blue Hat pumps his cock. For some reason, I find it incredibly hot that he doesn't even bother to push his pants down. Zipper open at the front, his jeans hug his perfect ass in the back as he fucks his friend's mouth. My throat dries, dying for a taste, dying for him to make demands of *me* like that while I'm on my knees.

While I'm happy for the two guys, and I really am, I'm also kind of jealous. That's the kind of passion I want to experience, the way I want to be talked to. Just once in my life, I want a man to devour me like that, to unleash himself on me…to *demand* I do things.

"That's enough," Blue Hat grunts, his rough voice low, nothing more than a whisper that drifts up to my ears in the quiet countryside. "Let me into that tight hole of yours."

Mr. Hottie goes back on his heels, and the man's huge cock slips from his mouth. With the back of his big hand, he wipes away the wet evidence glistening on his face and smiles up at the man he clearly adores. He unzips his pants, and shoves them to his knees, to expose his own big cock.

"Turn around," Blue Hat growls.

I can feel Mr. Hottie's excitement as he turns and goes down on all fours. Blue Hat wets his finger and slips it in his backside.

"Fuck yeah," Mr. Hottie says loudly, and Blue Hat slaps his ass.

"Jesus Christ, Luca. Do you want the fucking world to know what we're doing?"

Luca.

"Just fuck me already, then."

"Aww, what's the matter?" he asks as he spits on his finger and works another in, stretching the man and preparing him for his girth. "You've been hurting for my cock?" His voice is so low and deep I have to strain to hear.

"You know I have." He grunts and shifts on his knees. "You've been so busy we don't get a fucking minute alone anymore."

A bird flies overhead and slows, like it, too, wants a piece of the action. I give it a brief glance then concentrate on the act below, not wanting to miss a damn thing. Blue Hat finishes with the foreplay, grabs his cock in his big hand and grunts as he strokes it, once, twice, three times. On his knees, Mr. Hottie is working his own cock while the man about to ram home rips into a condom, sheathes himself and positions his crown at the opening. His ass clenches as he eases forward, offering only an inch at a time, and both men moan in bliss.

"Please," Mr. Hottie begs.

"You need me, Luca?"

"Yes," he murmurs and rears back, trying to get the man in deeper.

Blue Hat groans and presses down on Mr. Hottie's back to prevent him from moving. "Stay still," he commands through gritted teeth, letting the other man know exactly who's in charge of the depth and penetration.

And that is some very hot shit.

I lean farther over the rail and tremble from head to toe as the men fuck, coveting each other with a ferocity I've never seen before, but have always wanted. Blue Hat runs his hands through the other man's hair, fisting it and pulling his head back as he angles his body to get his cock in deeper. He seats himself high inside then pulls almost all the way out, only to slam back in again. Grunts and groans echo in my ears, and his hips jerk faster, with hard, blunt strokes that reach a maddening pace.

I'm dying. Seriously dying of lust overload here. Honest to God, I'm going to have to start watching man on man porn. The genuine way these guys want each other...well, that's seriously inspiring, and totally mind blowing.

I caress my clit, strum it like a finely tuned instrument, and my entire body goes up in a burst of flames as heat burns through my blood. I mouth the word yes, not daring to speak and break the moment as tension builds inside me. I apply more pressure to my clit and stroke harder, reaching a fevered pitch that has me soaring over the edge. Every muscle in my body clenches. My orgasm so powerful and blinding, I sink to my knees and lean forward to ride out the pleasure.

I stay like that for a long time, working to catch my breath as groans and a lot of curses reach my ears. When I'm finally able to see again, I peek down to catch Blue Hat throwing his head back. He's gripping the guy's hips for leverage and depleting himself inside.

"So fucking good," he groans.

The man on his knees shoots into his hand, then they both collapse on to the grass, rolling on their backs. I duck away as they break apart, my heart crashing so hard against my chest, I'm sure it's going to explode. That was...Jesus, I want to say amazing, but that doesn't even begin to describe the hunger they just displayed.

I hurry inside, quietly close the door behind me, and collapse on my bed, fanning my arms and legs out, desperate to cool my overheated, needy body. Outside the guys are talking quietly, but I can't hear their muffled whispers through my closed door. Exhaustion overtakes me, my eyes fall shut, the vision of the two of them groping each other still buzzing through my brain.

Why on earth can't I inspire that kind of passion in a guy?

All I ever get is sweet, gentle lovemaking. I am seriously so tired of the vanilla. Yeah, sure my dad is a minister, but come on, that doesn't mean I don't want to be forced to my knees and taken hard. If only I had it in me to open my mouth and just ask for what I want. I can't seem to do it, though. Probably because I've been lectured and browbeaten my whole life.

Sex is for procreating, Olivia. Anything out of the norm is socially unacceptable—wrong.

Dammit, I want wrong. The whole time I was with *him*, I'd wanted it wrong. What I wouldn't have given for my ex to do depraved things with me. But no, he treated me with respect, which meant slow, gentle sex the missionary way. Don't get me wrong. It was good, but I wanted more…needed more… had a deeper craving to be flipped over and corrupted.

I quiver as I think about that, and deep between my legs, my sex clenches one last time. Unfortunately, men see me as a nice girl. Respectable. Private and reserved. That's what you get when you're the daughter of a minister—a goddamn gentleman in bed.

I want a savage.

I want to be turned and twisted. I want to be ravaged and ridden. I want to be *made* to do things. Dirty things. Like watch two guys make out, then have them both take me— own me.

So what am I going to do about it?

Chapter Two

GIO

My leg bounces restlessly under the table as I glance at the freshly baked breads and the eggs, meats, and cheeses spread out on the linen before me. I lift my head, rake my hands through my hair, and meet my father's eyes—eyes that mirror my own—as it is in the Rossi family.

"Look," I begin for the hundredth time, even though I'm well aware that no matter what I say, no matter how many graphs and charts, how many brochures and ideas I present, I'll never be able to change my father's mind. The business is his to run, and he damn well plans to do things his way until I'm *allowed* to take over. "Business is declining rapidly. We need to make some big changes around here and draw in a younger crowd."

My father chews on a piece of buttered bread, takes a sip of his coffee, and looks at me thoughtfully. Beside him, my grandfather, with the same blue eyes—Mediterranean blue my ex, Olivia, use to call mine—keeps his focus on his food, but I know he's taking it all in, remaining quiet until he has something important to say.

"Son," Dad begins. "We've been over this. I understand you think you're ready to take over the business, make changes, but we follow tradition in this family. We have for hundreds of years, and we're not about to change that now."

For Christ's sake, I have a NYU business degree under my belt. I have what it takes to run the place, and I want a chance to do it and turn over a profit before we lose it all. When I left here for college years ago, I had planned to work at my uncle's marketing firm, but a situation with my girlfriend—or rather, ex-girlfriend now—had me returning. Since I've come home, business has been on a decline, and I can't stand to sit back and watch it happen. But until I marry, no way will the family let me take over and make changes—because that's how it is in the Rossi family.

Except marriage isn't in my future, not after walking out on the only girl I ever loved. I did it to protect her—from me. Yeah, I might be a good man, honorable, but when it comes to Olivia, I only have so much strength.

My mom sits down beside me, her gaze sympathetic, but she can't change my father's mind, either. Not that I think she wants to. No, she wants me married, too—a sign of maturity they say, which is ridiculous. Frustration builds inside me, and my leg shakes harder. Can't they see we could lose the place? Was being married and following tradition more important than keeping the villa that has been in our family for generations? Guess so, since my dad won't budge. So what the fuck am I supposed to do?

"What about Olivia, that nice girl you met in college?" Mom asks for the umpteenth time since I've returned home. Honest to fuck, I'm sick of her bringing up Olivia. It's over between us. And while I know she's trying to be helpful, I don't want to have this discussion right now. "You used to talk about her all the time when you came home for the holidays, and I've not seen you date anyone since you returned for good. I think you might still be holding out for her."

My entire body stiffens. Did my mother really think I was about to call my ex-girlfriend out of the blue, ask her to give up everything, move to Tuscany, and marry me? Yeah, like that's going to happen. Beside, she hates me, and even though I've never stopped thinking of her, never been able to get over her, she's too nice, too sweet for a guy like me. I did what I had to do to protect her, and that meant up and leaving when she talked about a future after college. I bite the inside of my mouth and try to block the haunted look she gave me when I left, the look that that still pains me to this day.

I try to swallow past the lump in my throat but I can't. *Shit, it still fucking hurts.*

"Whatever happened between you two, anyway?" Dad asks.

"Nothing," I say much too quickly, too harshly.

Grandpa lifts his head, and those blue Rossi eyes lock on mine. "So then, maybe you should think about it."

Grandpa and I have a stare off. Seconds turn into minutes, and I feel something inside me soften. Fuck, maybe he's right. Maybe I should call Olivia. Grandpa shouldn't be working the front counter because our tight budget can't afford new staff. The changes I want to make will draw in a new crowd, fresh blood, but I can't put any new plans in place if I'm not married. Stupid, fucking family tradition. My stomach tightens. Maybe I should call her, beg her to forgive me…hide the side of me that would surely frighten the hell out of a sweet girl like her.

"Yeah, I'll think about it," I say to appease them. I'm pretty sure my entire family knows about Luca and me, and while they seem to quietly accept what's between us, they really want me to take a wife. I wonder if it's important to them for tradition, or because they really know how much I care about Olivia. I wipe my mouth with my napkin and toss it onto the table. "If you'll excuse me, I have some business to attend to."

My mom and dad both nod, and their whispered words reach my ears as I step out of the dining room and make my way outside. I have a load of paperwork on my desk, but I need to talk to Luca. My best friend always knows the right things to say when I'm in a shit mood.

As the morning sunshine climbs the mountain, it does nothing to lighten my dark mood. I stretch out my arms and glance up the hill to see if Luca is inspecting the grapes. When my search comes up empty, I make my way to the winery. I open the doors and find him checking the temperatures on the stainless steel tanks.

Luca might be the same age as me, which is considered young for a vintner, but his family has been in the winemaking business for years. Someone from every generation has worked for the Rossi family for as long as anyone can remember. Luca and I had been friends since kindergarten, and just a few years ago, after his father retired, he took over as head vintner. At least he didn't have to get married to take the position.

Fuck. Fuck. Fuck.

"Hey," I say.

Dimples spread across his face as he sees me coming his way. "What's up?" he asks. Then he drops the clipboard to his side, frowning as his astute eyes move over me.

I scrub the scuff on my chin. "Yeah," is all I say.

He hooks a finger through my belt loop and drags me to him. I can already feel his cock growing, pressing against my groin. "What do you need?" he asks.

Jesus, I love the guy. One look at my sulking face and he's ready and willing to do whatever it takes to put a smile back on it. On the other side of the room, a few guys are working, and while there are lots of things Luca could do to take my mind off shit for thirty minutes or so, now is not the time or place.

I fist his hair, wrap it around my hand, and hold for a second. He waits for my command, but I let go and roughly push him off me. He backs off, no questions.

"I don't know what the fuck to do."

Luca nods. He knows what I'm talking about. We have no secrets. The first time we dared to kiss—at seventeen, our need for one another too strong to deny another second—we made a pact to always be honest.

"You're going to have to get married, dude. If you want to save this place, you have no choice."

I scoff. "No kidding."

"Why don't you call her?"

I shake my head. "Not you, too. Fuck, Luca."

Luca puts his hand on my shoulder. "Come on, you haven't met anyone else because you've been hung up on her for years. Maybe she still wants a future with you."

"She's a nice girl, Luca." I pause and wave my hand back and forth between the two of us. "This...I wouldn't want to keep it a secret from her, and as much as I'd kill to have her a part of it, she'd never understand." I draw a breath and let it out slowly as I stare at Luca. I've loved him for as long as I can remember. Quitting him would be like giving up breathing. He's one part of my soul. Olivia is the other. And while Luca accepts the side of me that needs to dominate and control, it would scare Olivia half to death.

"How do you know she wouldn't accept *all* sides of you?"

"I just do, okay."

"Stop the bullshit and answer the fucking question." My best friend has no trouble baring himself to me, letting me own him sexually, but outside the bedroom, he can be a cocky bastard who has no trouble pushing back. Truthfully, I wouldn't want it any other way.

"Sex with her was always sweet and tender. It was great because it was with her, but sooner or later I was going to break, order her around, and demand things of her."

"Like what?"

"Oh, like she lay herself across the mattress, breasts up, head dangling over the edge so I could shove my cock all the way down her throat and watch her take it." I swallow. Hard. "That's just one of the milder things I want to do with her."

I can feel my dick harden as I think about her in that position. Flat on her back, breasts in the air, my cock in her throat while Luca fucks her sweet pussy. *Luca…always in the scenario.*

"Jesus. She's just not that kind of girl, and I don't want to be the one to corrupt her. Besides, I'll bet my left nut she'd hang up if I tried to call."

I scrub my jaw and clench down hard enough to break teeth, hating how much I'd hurt her when I walked away. It was the last thing I ever wanted to do, which was why I left in the first place.

Luca returns his focus to his work and checks something on the steel take. As he writes on the clipboard, he says, "Maybe she'd be into all this."

I shrug, but Luca isn't looking at me. "Doubtful."

"You won't know until you try."

"Luca…"

He turns back to me, his eyes serious, like he's had enough of my shit for the day. "Okay, find someone else and marry them already, before you lose the fucking vineyard."

"If my parents thought for one minute that I was faking a marriage, they'd never sign the papers over."

"Fine, then. Make a deal with Olivia. Tit for tat. You give her something she needs in exchange for being your wife. Your parents will believe that marriage is real since you've been obsessing over her for years. You get the papers, and in one year, or less, or however the fuck long, you break up. If you don't lay a hand on her, you won't be tempted to do the darker things you want."

I look at him as I chew on his idea. Ludicrous? Yes. But Jesus, it just might work. It's not like I haven't kept track of her over the years. I know she's stuck in a shitty, dead-end job in Seattle. She hates the rain, so why she went to Seattle after NYU is beyond me. Then again, she probably went halfway across the country to get as far away from me as possible. But one call to my uncle in New York and I'd have her working in a firm that respects her.

"It's not a bad idea," I say.

"Good. Decision made. Make it happen."

"You know if this happened, you and I…" I stop to really drive the point home. "We can't."

"I know."

"I love the fuck out of you Luca, you know that, but I'm not a cheater. Even if the marriage is fake."

His smile is slow, and his eyes darken. "I love the fuck out of you, too, Gio. Nothing is going to change that. I've always accepted that you loved Olivia, too. She's a part of you, which makes her a part of me, too."

I fist my hair. "The only way we could be together is if it was the three of us, and that's not going to happen."

Luca steps up to me and lowers his voice. "Listen, you have to do what you have to do save this place. That's the priority. As for us, I have a feeling things will work out the way they're supposed to."

He turns from me, and I take in his swagger as he walks away, moving from tank to tank. With my thoughts racing a million miles an hour, I head to the fields. If I called her, would she even talk to me? I walk along the rows of grapes, stopping to examine a few, the idea of seeing Olivia again both exciting and frightening. I catch a warm, familiar scent, a mix of vanilla and honey. It takes me back to happier times when I was in Olivia's bed. But I'm only recalling the scent because she's at the forefront of my brain.

I walk to the next row of vines, and when the scent grows stronger, I look up from the plants I'm examining. I freeze, as my blood stops flowing and my lungs seize.

No. Fucking. Way.

I blink, sure I'm hallucinating. No way in hell would Olivia be standing in my vineyard tossing grapes in the air and catching them in her mouth—the sweet, pouty mouth that I'd love to feel wrapped around my cock. It can't be a coincidence. I don't believe in them. There has to be something bigger at work here, something that has reunited us when I needed her most.

"Olivia?" She turns slowly, and even though she's too focused on catching the grapes and doesn't realize it's me yet, I say, "Marry me."

A gasp of surprise catches in her throat as the round fruit slides in, lodging itself deep and blocking her airflow. Her eyes go wide as she grasps her neck.

Oh Jesus.

Chapter Three

OLIVIA

I can't breathe.

Oh my God. I'm going to die. I work to suck in air, but all I do is draw the grape in deeper. Gio spins me around—at least I think it's Gio—and his strong hands circle my stomach. He gives hard, upward thrusts, but as my vision fades, I'm sure this is it—and to die without having awesome sex really sucks. My life flashes before my eyes, and I'm not even sure it's worth watching until I see him. I've reached the end. No way, no how could he be here, right?

Another hard thrust dislodges the grape, and it shoots from my mouth like a cork from a bottle. I'd be embarrassed if I wasn't so happy to be alive. I gasp and fill my lungs, reveling in the fresh country air. My heart rate begins to slow, my vision expanding, and I turn to see my savior—then again, I probably wouldn't have choked on the grape had he not called my name and asked me to marry him.

Marry me.

A tremble moves through me as I take in the most gorgeous blue eyes I've ever seen. "Gio?" I say cautiously, still not sure if I'm dead or not.

"Yeah," he says softly. "It's me. You okay?"

"I…what…" I falter backward, and with lightning fast reflexes he slides an arm around my waist, dragging me to him. I sag against his hard body, and everything in the way he's holding me is so familiar…so right. "Gio," I say again then pinch my eyes shut, expecting him to be gone when I open them again. But no, he's standing over me, looking down with stormy blue eyes I fear I could get lost in again. Oh God, I still love him.

Get it together, Olivia. He broke your heart.

I push at his chest and try to break away, my pulse slamming so hard against my neck, it's hard to keep a clear thought.

"What are you doing here?" I finally ask, hating that my voice is as shaky as my hands.

"I'm the one who should be asking you that."

I shake my head and look around. "Is this…yours?"

He examines the vast vineyard with me, and I see the pride in his eyes. "Yes, this is my home, Olivia."

"I can't believe this." He tilts his head and touches a strand of my hair, and it takes every bit of strength I possess to push his hand way.

"What are you doing here?" he asks.

"I'm on vacation. I didn't know this was your place." As blood rages through my body, I step farther away, but stop when my back connects with a grapevine. How can this be happening? Of all the vineyards in Italy, I end up at Gio's? I mean, I knew his family owned a vineyard somewhere in Italy, but it's a big country, and I figured chances of my sponsor sending me to his were slim to none. Well, apparently not, since I'm currently standing on his property, staring up at him.

"So you're telling me this *is* a coincidence?" he asks.

I look down, stare at the grass beneath my feet, as I consider my dossier. I go over everything in my mind, and my stomach clenches. Slowly, I lift my head, and my heart catches when I find him still staring at me. "No," I say, hardly able to believe one of my best friends set this up on purpose. Why would she do that? They all know how much I hate Gio. "This trip was a birthday gift, and I think I was sent here on purpose."

"Olivia," he says softly and takes a step toward me, his scent messing with my body and brain. "This was meant to be."

Marry me.

Did he really ask me that, or was that just wishful thinking on my part?

"Gio?"

"Yeah."

"Did you…" I stop speaking. If I ask and I'm wrong, I'm going to come across like an idiot.

"Did I what?"

"Nothing."

His smile is slow, sexy, and for a guy who wanted no future with me, he sure is looking at me like he wants to devour me.

Oh how I wish.

"If you're wondering if I just asked you to marry me, the answer is yes."

My heart races—okay, gallops—as I try to process his words. Honest to God, I can't believe Gio is standing in front of me, asking me to marry him. I suck in a sharp breath and struggle to fuel my brain, as his presence dominates my senses. Jesus, what I wouldn't have done to hear those two little words on his lips two years ago.

But he didn't just break my heart, he tore it from my chest and kicked it around all the way back to Italy.

"I can't believe — " I begin, but he presses his finger to my lips to stop me. My heart flutters as he takes control, and I hate my body's reaction. I briefly shut my eyes and remind myself I hate him.

"Hear me out." He holds his finger more firmly against my lips, waiting. I nod and his hand drops. "I know you hate me, and I don't blame you. But I need a favor." I open my mouth to ask why I'd do him any favors, when a shake of his head stops me. "You see this?" He waves his hands around the vineyard. "Beautiful, right?" I nod. "It's been in the family for generations, and if I don't do something, we're going to lose it."

"What does that have to do with asking me to marry you?" I blurt out.

His eyes go stormy again, and he exhales sharply as he thrusts a hand through his hair. "Family tradition. The oldest son takes over the business, but he must be married first."

As he explains, I don't know whether I want to laugh or cry. One thing I do know is that I'm glad I didn't scream *yes* at his proposal. How foolish would I have felt when I found out the real reason he wanted my hand in matrimony?

"You need a wife to save the vineyard?" I ask, still trying to wrap my brain around all this. He needs a damn wife. No way in hell is it going to be me.

He drives his hands into his jeans and they drop lower on his hips. I try not to stare, but he's so gorgeous, even more so with two years of hard muscles added to his once thinner frame. His hair is cut short, the dark color accentuating the blue in his eyes. A light gray T-shirt is snug against broad shoulders and hard abs that I used to go crazy over.

He broke your heart.

Jesus, how many times did I have to remind myself of that? "Why would I ever do anything for you?" I ask, keeping my voice steady and cool.

He dips his head. "I would never ask for something

without giving in return." His eyes darken, and I have to wonder exactly what it is he wants to give me. Can he read the need in my eyes, the want?

How much my heart still aches for him?

"Go on," I say, trying for casual when my insides are in total chaos.

"I can help you get out of that dead-end job you're in. One call and you could be working at East Coast Media."

I gasp, partly because his uncle's firm is where I always wanted to work, and partly because he knows what's been going on in my life.

I glare at him. "How do you know where I work?"

"I've been keeping tabs."

He's been keeping tabs on me? Why the hell would a man who dumped me do that? I stare at his chest and shake my head. I don't know whether to feel violated or pleased. Either way, what I do know is I can't—won't—pretend to be his... anything. Not after everything we've been through.

"No," I say. "I can't do this."

"This is all coming at you rather fast. I'm sorry about that, Olivia. I'm just…desperate."

"Why me. Why now? There are plenty of women in Italy who would say yes to you. I mean look at you." As soon as the words leave my mouth, I stumble and try to gobble them back up. "I…I just don't know why you asked me."

"Because I know you." He touches me again, runs the back of his knuckles down my arm. I shiver, and I want to step away but can't seem to make myself do it. "It needs to be believable. My parents aren't going to sign over the vineyard if they think I'm marrying just to get my hands on it. With you, it will be believable."

"I don't know why you think that. You ran—"

"It just will be, okay. Trust me on that."

He wants me to trust him. Fat chance.

"So what exactly would you want me to do?" I ask, curiosity getting the better of me, even though I'm never going to do whatever it is.

"We'll have a fast ceremony here on the hill tomorrow. Just my mom and dad and grandfather."

"Tomorrow?" I stare at a bird as it flies overhead, and try to wrap my brain around all this. He actually wants me to go through with a ceremony? That's insane! "Your parents are not going to believe any of this."

"I think they will, especially since they asked about you earlier, and then you happened to just show up."

My head jerks up. "Why would they ask about me?"

He goes quiet for a long time and pinches the bridge of his nose, his expression one of pure and perfect agony. "Because I've always cared about you, Olivia. I've never stopped."

I push down the hurt and square my shoulders. "Just not enough to plan a future with me," I respond, finally understanding why he just upped and left two days after I talked about a future. But as I look at him now, I get the sense there is more to it than that.

"It wasn't…it's not like…" He takes a quick breath and lets it out slowly. "I'll tell them you came looking for me," he says, redirecting the conversation. "And the second I saw you, I knew it was fate bringing us back together."

A strange noise sounds in my throat. "But it wasn't," I counter. "It was my friend."

"They don't need to know that. They believe in fate and will believe that you came looking for me because we were meant to be together forever."

My stomach clenches. Oh God, how I had wanted that to be true. But it's too late for that now.

"How long are you here?" he asks.

"Three weeks."

"Plenty of time. You stay with me for those weeks, then

when your trip is over, you can fly back home, claim it didn't work out. We can get an annulment. No one would ever have to know."

I'd know.

"Don't worry. It will all be just an act, Olivia. It will be in name only, and once the vineyard is signed over to me, we'd no longer have to put on a show."

I look at him, taking in the frown lines around his mouth, the worry and fear ghosting his eyes. "This is important to you, isn't it?"

Jesus, girl, you can't seriously be considering this!

He nods, and my heart misses a beat.

Oh cripes, I can feel myself caving. *Stay strong, Olivia— pretending to be his wife, sharing a bed for the next few weeks with him not being yours, will be emotional suicide. I should just slice open a vein and bleed out now.* I shake my head. I can't. I just can't.

"Gio—"

"We'd be helping each other out."

I think about the job at East Coast Media. I'd do just about anything to work for a firm that respects the women it employs. "One thing," I say, hardly able to believe what I'm about to do.

"Name it."

"You get me the interview. I get the job on my own merit."

He nods. "One more thing for me, too."

Anything...

Oh God, Olivia you are so pathetic.

"What's that?"

"I want you to help me. I'd love to put our brains together, come up with ideas on how to market this place to a younger crowd."

Brains together...bodies together.

"What do you say, Olivia?"

Chapter Four

OLIVIA

Why on earth did I ever say yes? I must be some sort of masochist. It's the only explanation. When this is over, I'm going to wake up in a cold bed feeling like I'd had one too many shots of Patron. Again.

I sneak a sideways glance at the man beside me as he drives along the winding road leading to town. My heart thumps a little as I take in his features. Square jaw, firm chin, hard body that fills me with want. He turns my way, but I'm too slow to react and he catches me staring.

How can I still love him so much?

"Everything okay?" he asks, his hand sliding across the seat to capture mine. He gives a small squeeze, and my lungs constrict with it.

"I'm okay," I squeak, even though I'm not. I can't believe that in a few short hours I'll be marrying the man I never stopped loving, even though his departure took the wind out of me and I haven't been able to breathe quite the same since.

I glance at my purse and think about texting one of the girls. Would they talk me out of this, tell me I'm absolutely crazy? Which I probably am. Or would they tell me to go for it, enjoy the rights that go with marriage? Needing a distraction, something else to mull over as we drive to town to pick out a dress for the ceremony, I think about my brief meeting with his parents after agreeing to his ludicrous plan.

"Your parents are nice, Gio. I like them a lot."

His mouth curves as he takes a corner. "They like you a lot, too."

I smooth my hand over the fuchsia sundress I'm wearing and stretch out my legs, admiring my Jimmy Choos. They don't go with the outfit, but I don't care. I paid a shitload of money for them and planned to wear them every chance I had. Then again, maybe I'm wearing them because I know high heels are one of Gio's fetishes.

That's not going to make him love you again, Olivia.

"I can't believe they bought it when you told them I came looking for you."

"I can. They know I still care about you."

Just not enough to plan a future.

At that painful thought, which nearly shatters my heart, I turn back to the window and take in the gorgeous countryside. I swallow the knot in my throat so I can talk with clarity. "I can see why you wanted to move back here. This place is gorgeous. And I understand the villa is important to you." More important than me, obviously. But I don't say that.

"Liv," he begins, then stops abruptly.

My gaze jerks back to his.

Liv.

The shortening of my name feels like a hard slap to the face. He only ever called me Liv when we were in bed, sharing intimacies, and this marriage isn't about love. He doesn't want me sexually. Had made it clear he wants a wife in name only.

"What?" I finally ask.

He clenches his jaw, the muscles so tight I think they might snap. "Tell me more about this birthday present," he says, once again redirecting the conversation.

"Well," I begin. "Harper thought it would be fun to do something epic on each of our twenty-fifth birthdays, so we all put our names in a hat." Gio nods as I continue with the explanation, and when I get to the part about sex, he slowly turns my way.

"You're supposed to just sleep with some random guy?"

"Yeah, something like that."

He shakes his head. "Jesus."

"What?"

He frowns and says, "Nothing. We're here."

I follow his gaze and see the sprawling mall. The Prada and Gucci logos draw my attention. The gorgeous stone and glass building with the designer boutiques is pretty high end. I shift uneasily. Gio must pick up on it because he squeezes my hand again.

"Anything you want," he says. "On me."

"I just want something simple. No sense in spending a lot on a fake wedding, right?"

His nod is tight as he slides from the car and comes around my side to escort me out. I sigh at his chivalry. He's always the gentleman when it comes to me. And while I like that outside the bedroom…inside is a very different story. My mind briefly flashes back to the two men devouring each other behind my villa, and a hot tingle spreads through my body and settles deep between my legs. I haven't seen Mr. Hottie since that incident, and I've been searching high and low for the guy who wore the blue hat.

He captures my hands and weaves his fingers through mine in a familiar way. We fit together so easily, it's hard to believe two years have passed. But they have, and this isn't real. Heat splashes over me as we walk to the building, my shoes clicking on the sidewalk. As we approach the main entrance, the doors peel open to invite us in, and the air conditioning crashes over us like a cool wave. Delightful.

Gio guides me to the directory, looks it over, and frowns. "Where to first?" he asks, and I get it. He's out of his element.

I smile, and for a moment think about dragging this shopping trip out, punishing him a little. Payback for leaving me? Yeah, probably. Torturous for him? Definitely. But I don't follow through, because we're short on time, and maybe I just can't be that mean to the man who owns my heart.

I point to the store that carries bridal gowns. I don't want anything fancy, and it has to fit me off the rack because we don't have time for anything else. "Let's go here."

Gio maps the path and guides me through the throngs of shoppers bustling about, numerous bags in hand. We step into the store and a sales lady around my age greets us.

"*Buongiorno*. Good Morning," she says in both Italian and English, probably because the store caters to locals and tourists alike. Her teeth flash in a smile as she looks me over, sizes me up.

"Good morning," I respond.

"What can I help you with today?" she asks in English.

"I need a dress. I'm getting married in…" I pause and glance at my watch. "Four hours."

"Oh my goodness," she says, and zeros in on my stomach. She obviously thinks I'm pregnant. I resist the urge to correct her.

Gio, however, pulls me into his arms, a public display of affection. "We've been apart," he says and cups my chin. He dips his head, his lips so close to mine I'm sure he's going to kiss me.

Please kiss me. My pulse thumps, and my lips part in offering.

"And I'm not waiting another second to make this beautiful woman mine," he says quietly, like he's speaking only to me.

My heart leaps. There's something so deep and honest in his eyes as he looks at me, if I didn't know better, I would think he is serious.

But I do know better.

He hovers over me for a moment, and when the kiss doesn't come, I blink to pull myself together. I straighten and try to get my breathing under control as the sales lady smiles at Gio, then gives him the once over. Twice. Jealousy surges inside me, and I want to tell her to back the hell off, he's spoken for. But I don't because, really, he isn't. Still, to eye-fuck a guy while his bride—fake or not—is beside him is crude. If my girlfriend Harper were here, she'd have punched the chick by now.

"Please come with me. I think I have just the dress for you."

Gio keeps his arm around me in a possessive, loving way that envelops me in warmth and feels much deeper than pretend—deeper than just "caring about me."

If only...

"What was that all about?" I ask.

"I didn't like the condescending way she looked at your stomach. Pregnant or not, it's none of her fucking business, and I protect what is mine."

What is mine?

I swallow the knot clogging my throat and follow the sales lady to the back of the store. The hangers scrape the metal rod as she searches through the dresses. She casts another glance my way. "Size six?"

"Yes," I say, and she pulls a simple, strapless, A-line dress from the rod and displays it for me. "I think this will be beautiful on you."

I look it over and glance at Gio. "What do you think?"

His knuckles brush mine, the touch powerful and intimate, so goddamn real I pinch my leg to remind myself it's not. "Anything will be beautiful on you, Olivia," he whispers in the softest voice.

Good God, if he keeps touching me and looking at me like that, I'll never survive this.

I run shaky fingers over the dress. "It's so pretty."

"Try it on," Gio says, looking like he's in total agony as he gives my hand a little squeeze. I pause for a second and take in his pained expression. What the hell has come over him? I'm about to ask but stop when he gestures toward the changing room and says, "Go."

"Okay."

I make a move to turn, but his hand captures mine to stop me. "Liv," he says, his voice a soft rasp that sends shivers skittering through me. "I want to see it on you."

The sales lady wags her finger at Gio. "Now, you know it's bad luck for the groom to see the bride in her dress, right?"

"Yeah, I know." He drops onto the sofa facing the changing rooms. I meet his eye, and he gives me a smile so full of heat and promise, my entire body warms. "I'm waiting," he says.

I slip into the changing room and peel off my sundress. My fingers slide over the soft silk of the dress, as I put my feet into it and pull it up. I press my hand to my stomach and turn left and right, the hem swishing with the movement. So far I love it, but I can't quite seem to get it zipped all the way. I open the door in search of help, and when I find Gio staring at me from the sofa, his eyes flaring hot, my knees wobble. My God, is it possible that he *does* want me in his bed?

Could he want me as much as I want him?

I mull that over for a second then bite the inside of my cheek as I give myself a quick lecture. *This isn't about love or sex. You're both just doing each other a favor, Olivia.*

"Need a hand?" he asks, his voice deeper, rougher than it was before.

I turn and gather my hair to expose my back. "Yeah. The zipper."

The leather chair makes a squishing sound as he rises, then he closes the distance between us. I watch him in the mirror as his gaze goes to my exposed back. Warm knuckles brush my skin, his movement slow and deliberate as he pulls the zipper up, the teeth cutting the sudden tension between us. For a second, I envision our wedding night, and Gio sliding the zipper down instead of pulling it up. My entire body tightens as I conjure up the image, and my breasts grow heavy, needy, aching for something rough and greedy from Gio.

He meets my gaze in the mirror and holds it. "Beautiful," he says, the heat from his mouth washing over my bare shoulders. My sex clenches as the warmth from his breath trickles downward, stopping to play with every erogenous zone on the way.

This might be an act, a hands-off marriage to fool his parents, but heck, maybe I should change his mind on that. I mean, I'm not supposed to go home until I've had sex, right? Maybe I should take advantage of this situation and seduce the guy I'm about to marry.

Heartache is something I avoid, and I don't plan to ever trust him again, but since this man already shattered my heart, what more could he do to it? What more do I have to lose? Seducing my husband makes perfect sense, and then at least I'll be fulfilling my part of the New Years Eve pact.

And maybe, just maybe, I'll summon the courage to tell him how I really want him to take me in bed.

Chapter Five

Gio

After a very fast ceremony on the vineyard, I pace around the honeymoon suite in the main castle, my cock so hard it's all I can do to remind myself Olivia is my wife in name only. She's not mine to strip bare, toss on the bed, and have my wicked fucking way with. We're simply doing each other a favor, and I'd be wise to remember that.

But that doesn't stop me from wanting to do dirty things with her. For two long years, I thought about her, wanted her, craved her with an intensity that frightened me a little. And today, seeing her in her curve-hugging white dress, looking so gorgeous as the minister united the two of us in front of my three family members—Luca watching as well—pretty much had me teetering on the edge of sanity.

I pull the curtains open and crack the window, hoping the cooler night air will clear my head. When the bathroom door creaks open, I turn to see Olivia coming my way. She's dressed in a sexy little white lace number that arouses the beast in me, and I'm afraid that not even the night air will help cage my lust.

Seriously, though. Is she fucking trying to kill me? Christ, she knows white lace is my favorite, and if I didn't know better, I'd think she was trying to fuck with my last working brain cell. I grunt. Maybe this is her way of retaliating after I turned my back on her.

She shrugs, her eyes apologetic. "This is all I have," she explains. "It came with the dossier."

Right, the dossier. Okay, so, no way could she be fucking with me on purpose. She wasn't even the one who'd packed her clothes. I nod and try to keep my cool as she walks to the bed, a little extra shake in her hips—or maybe I imagine that—and slides under the covers.

I shut the curtains, but leave the window open, my thoughts going to the pact she'd described. I still can't believe sleeping with some random stranger was a part of the deal. If she wants someone to sleep with, it damn well should be me.

Don't go there, dude.

"Why do you think your friend sent you here, to my villa?"

Still dressed in my tux from the ceremony, I shrug out of the jacket and yank off my tie. Olivia's eyes track my every movement. Christ, if she keeps looking at me with those big doe's eyes of hers, no way can I be held accountable for my actions.

"I have no idea," she says, fixing the blankets around her. "But I plan to find out when I return in three weeks."

Did her friend think we had unfinished business? Send Olivia to me on purpose? If so, she was right. But there's nothing I can do about it. Olivia is a good girl in the purest form, and I'm not about to corrupt her. I walk across the room and pour another scotch. Alcohol might be the only thing to help me get through this night without ravaging an innocent.

I hold the cup out to her. "Drink?"

She presses her palm to her forehead. "No, I'm still feeling the effects from all the champagne we drank." She looks around the room. "So this is the honeymoon suite. It's nice, but where do you usually sleep?"

"I have a room in the main castle here. But now that we're married, we'll move into one of the villas. It's tradition."

"I'm actually booked into one of those villas. Abrusco."

I freeze. "Granddad put you there?"

She nods.

Shit. That place hadn't been rented out in months. Since it's isolated from the main castle, as well as the other villas, and no one ever goes there, it's where Luca and I meet to get a little privacy around this place. Either there or in the cellar of the winery where we keep our family's private reserve. We can't very well go to my room in the main house, and he lives five miles down the road. Was it possible...? Fuck, no. No way could she have seen or heard us, or she would have said something.

Her fingers leave her forehead to race through her hair, and as her long, dark curls fall over her back, my focus shifts and I envision her straddling my body, Luca behind her, the two of us taking her until she's screaming our names.

Stop it.

I quickly wipe that image from my mind and down the rest of the dark liquid in my glass. It burns my throat as I reach for the button on my pants.

"What are you doing?" she asks, her gaze briefly dropping to my fingers before dashing upward.

"Getting out of these clothes." I meet her flickering gaze. "I sleep naked, remember."

"I remember," she whispers, her voice so low I have to strain to hear it.

Pink stains her cheeks, making her look so angelic. "I'm

sorry," I say. *What the fuck were you thinking, dude?* "I'll keep my clothes on."

"No. It's okay." She waves her hands and then lets them fall to her sides. "This is just so surreal. When I came here, I never thought I'd run into you, or find myself in a fake marriage, sleeping in the honeymoon suite. It's a lot to take in."

My heart pinches as I look at her, and all I want to do is go to her, comfort her—tell her how much I fucking love her, how much I want this to be real. But I can't do that. Not without eventually ruining her. In an effort to lessen her worries, and keep the beast leashed, I point to the chair in the corner. "I can sleep there."

She wets her bottom lip, and my insides coil tight. That's one of my biggest turn-ons, that and high heels, and she damn well knows it. I study her. Is it possible that she wants me? That she is going out of her way to seduce me?

Doesn't matter. I'm not going there. I can't.

"It's not like we haven't shared a bed," she says and sinks lower into the mattress, her body writhing and making me bat-shit crazy as she settles herself.

My mind instantly goes back to the times I had her beneath me, and I shift so she doesn't see the state of my cock. "Yeah, I know. But—"

"Let's just get some sleep, okay." She pats the side of the bed. "We're both adults and know the score."

She thinks she knows the score? Not fucking likely. The carnal side of me fights not to cross a line, push her past her comfort zone, and show her. But I wrestle that side into submission as I circle the bed.

"Yeah, okay," I mumble.

Body hard and tense, I shed the rest of my clothes, all but my shorts. No need to free the beast and make this situation worse. I make a quick trip to the bathroom then slide between the sheets. Liv's sweet, vanilla scent reaches my nostrils, and I breathe her in then cough to cover the growl rumbling in my throat.

"You okay?"

Okay? Hell no. I'm pretty sure I'll never be okay again.

"Yeah."

"'Kay. G'night."

"Night."

I roll, putting my back to her and resist the urge to shove my shorts to my knees and take my cock into my hands. The muscles along my jaw twitch as I clench hard, fighting my natural inclination to touch her. As I will sleep to come, I occupy my mind with the villa and all the changes I want to make to bring it into the twenty-first century and turn the place into a thriving resort. Beside me, Olivia shifts restlessly, and I wish to fuck she'd stop moving, stop reminding me she is there.

"Gio," she asks quietly.

Don't answer. Don't answer.

"Yeah?"

"Why…"

I wait for her to continue. When she doesn't I ask, "Why what?"

She goes quiet for a long time. "I'm really happy you're going to take ownership of the villa. What do you plan to do to it?"

"I want to bring in a younger crowd. Liven the place up a bit."

"When I first arrived, I was thinking the same thing."

My leg touches hers, and she exhales a fluttery breath. It washes over me as I turn her way, even though facing her is against my best interests. "Yeah?"

Her eyes meet mine in the dim room. "I thought I was going to be bored to death here."

Don't touch her, Gio.

"And now?" I ask, my hand slowly sliding across the small space between us, drawn by a force I don't seem to have any control over. Fuck me. "You don't think that now?"

"I'm kind of excited to put together a marketing plan. See what we can do together. It will definitely look good on my resume if we can get this place thriving."

"You've always had a brilliant mind, Olivia." And a gorgeous body. One, even though I know better, I can't seem to keep my hands off of.

The tip of my index finger touches her stomach, and I practically stop breathing when she tightens. The air around us charges with sexual energy, and my cock grows another inch.

"So this pact," I begin slowly, not wanting to scare her off as I play with the lace on her sexy underwear. "You said you weren't supposed to go home until you've had sex, right?"

What the fuck are you doing, dude?

"Yeah, but not just sex. *Epic* sex." She makes a strange noise as her eyes slide away, like she can't look at me, like she's holding some sort of secret. Dammed if I don't want to find out what it is. "Crazy, right?"

"Maybe. But I was thinking."

Stop. Just stop and roll the fuck away already.

"About?" she asks.

"I could help you with that." I slide my hand to her waist and shift closer, wanting to corrupt her, to own her completely.

Keep it together, Gio.

Her eyes snap back to mine, and I swallow against the dryness in my throat. "You could?" she asks, heat flashing in her dark eyes. Jesus Christ, she might hate me for running out on her, but she wants me as much as I want her.

"Yeah, I mean, it's not like I've never been inside you," I say, and her breathing becomes more erratic. Fuck, I shouldn't be doing this, but after two long years of wanting her, I don't have the strength to fight it anymore. "And I don't like the idea of you in some strange guy's bed."

That vision actually fills me with white-hot rage.

She lifts her chin, despite the rapid-fire breathing, the heat of her body, the desire reflected in her dark eyes—all signs she wants this—and says, "This arrangement doesn't come with rights, Gio. It's fake. Plus I can take care of myself." Her protest is so fucking weak. I wonder what kind of game she's playing.

Time to find out.

"Yeah, well, this isn't fake." Gone too far to turn back now, I take her hand and put it on my cock. As she closes her fingers around it, I pinch my eyes shut, and work to keep a measure of calm when all I want to do is crash over her, launch into her, take her the way I've always longed to.

"Gio," she whispers, but I close my mouth over hers and swallow her feeble protest. At first, her lips are firm, hesitant, but I buck into her hand, and she softens. It takes every ounce of strength I possess to leash the beast inside me. I bite back a curse, and as she kisses me back, drawing my tongue into her mouth, a rush of tenderness steals over me. Good. That's what she needs from me. Soft, easy lovemaking. Not a filthy animal who wants to bend her over and do dirty things to her.

Always protective of her, I rein in my lust and break the kiss to press my mouth to the hollow of her neck, licking the sensitive spot that always drives her crazy. She writhes beneath my mouth, and the softness of her skin, such a contrast to Luca's roughness, damn near shuts down my mind. But I draw a fueling breath to keep my last working brain cell functioning. She trembles, and I slide down her body, tug on her lace, and take one hard nipple into my mouth. I flatten my tongue and lick, laving her gently, and her hands go to my hair.

She grips my head and holds me to her, stroking my cock as her legs widen, her sweet pussy calling out to me. "Please..." she begs, a note of desperation in her tone.

I tear my mouth from her puckered nipple and look up at her. Her gaze clashes with mine, and I see something in the depths of her eyes. "Please, what?" I ask. Normally she's quiet during sex, more docile than this.

"I...I..." she begins, then drops her head back onto the pillow. She tosses her head from side to side, her hair fanning out as she trembles with a need I'd never seen in her before. Maybe her near death experience had done something to her. "Please," she says again.

I freeze for a moment, and my muscles tighten. What exactly is she begging me for? All she has to do is tell me and I'll give it to her.

"Olivia?" I ask, but she takes my head in her hands and guides my mouth back to her breasts. I slide my tongue over her bare skin, and pay homage to her nipple before I switch to the other breast, unable to get enough of her. I nibble her and eat at her as lust burns through my body, making me forget what it was I wanted to ask. Driven by need, I cup her breasts. Greedy bastard that I am, I clamp down on her taut bud—not as hard as I would have liked.

"Gio," she whimpers, her voice tight.

Easy, dude.

I lick softly to ease the sting, then kiss the underside of her swells, lick her lightly scented skin, and when she moans, my dick jumps.

I work not to crush her under my weight as I begin a slow journey downward, and close my eyes against the flood of heat urging me to strip her naked, have her at my mercy. Fuck, what I'd do to shove my cock down her throat, watch her open her mouth wide for me and take me deeper than ever before. But I won't do that because she's a good girl.

With need urging me on, I grip her thighs and stretch them wide. Using my teeth, I tear at the sexy white lace preventing me from ravishing her. The sound of material ripping cuts through me, but it's her gasp of shock that reminds me this is sweet Olivia.

"I'll replace them," I whisper, as her hips rise to meet my mouth.

"Gio," she whispers and moves against my face, grinding her sweet pussy against my chin. My heart thunders, the scent of her arousal wrapping around my aching cock and stroking furiously. Fuck, I need to come, to drive inside and lose myself in her wet heat. But first I need to bury my face in her gorgeous cunt and make her come in my mouth. I want to taste her sweet release, drink her in.

I shift positions and shove her knees to her breasts, then push outward, so she's wide open for me, mine to take any fucking way I want. "Keep your legs like this," I say gruffly, and she grips them to hold them up. I look her over, and my mouth salivates when I see moisture glistening on her sex. It's insane how much I miss fucking her, even if I have to control myself. My cock throbs with renewed pleasure as her sweet scent saturates the air.

"You have the prettiest pussy," I say, brushing her sex gently, but when my fingers come back soaking wet, my control snaps. Forgetting chivalry, I drive my finger into her slick warmth and stroke so fucking deep her pussy clenches. I shove another finger in, even though I want my mouth there. As I tease and torment the hot bundle of nerves inside her tight body, my muscles ripple as she closes around me, squeezes the hell out of my fingers. Christ, she's still so fucking snug I'm never going to last.

Her breathing grows shallow, and she moves, shifting on the mattress, and while this is a new side to her, I want her still, helpless beneath me. I want her at my mercy. My heart crashes harder, and I withdraw my fingers to flip her over. She squeals in surprise, and with thoughts that are anything but pure, I squeeze her ass, massaging her cheeks before I spread her wide. I want to smack her ass, bite it, leave it red and stinging by the time I'm done with her.

Instead, I shove a pillow under her hips and resist my darker urges as her pussy opens wide. Desperate for a taste, I lean in and lick her. That first sweet touch of my tongue to her heat sets off a chain of events inside my body, and if I don't fuck her soon I'm going to explode. Starting at her clit, I drag my tongue to her tight opening. Teetering on the edge, I shove my tongue inside and fuck her with it. Hard blunt strokes turn a whimper into a soft cry that lets me know how close she is. Her cunt tightens and sucks my tongue in and the storm raging inside me reaches a catastrophic level.

"Stay still," I bite out, unable to stop myself. "Or I'll tie you down."

She goes still, and I curse under my breath. Fuck, I scared her. I lick her again, bring her attention back to her sweet pussy and the need building inside her. Focusing on her pleasure, I lick, taste, and plunge inside. Fuck, I want to spend the night between her legs, want to eat her, feast on her until morning, but my balls are aching like a son of a bitch.

With her breasts crushed against the bed, I give another lick, her sounds of pleasure pushing me over the edge. She moans, and I thrust a finger harder, deeper…a little rougher.

Her ass rises, straining toward me. The position is a dangerous one and frays the last of my control. I slide my hand down until I reach her back passage. I insert my pinky, and for a second she freezes in what I can only assume is trepidation. I wait it out, wait for her to scurry away. When she doesn't, I move it a little and suck her clit between my teeth. She whimpers and lust roars through me.

Easy, Gio. One finger doesn't mean she wants the same

things you do.

Her ass is so tight. I can tell she's never had anal before. Fuck, that thrills me. I want to be the guy to introduce her. I let her get used to the feel, then shove my other hand between her body and the pillow and crush her clit with the base of my palm. A broken gasp crawls out of her throat.

"Come for me, Liv," I whisper from between her legs, and as soon as the words leave my mouth, she lets go. Her body clenches once, twice, three times, and I stay put, lapping her sweet honey, not wanting to miss a single drop. So sweet. So fucking sweet.

When I have her clean, I go back on my heels to see her. She turns, and half-closed eyes meet mine. The euphoric look on her face makes me impossibly harder. I'm about to crawl back up her body and drive my cock home, when she sits up, pulls my shorts to my thighs, and takes my cock into her mouth.

"Jesus, fuck," I growl, and grab a fistful of her hair, wrapping it around my hand three times.

She fills her mouth, tasting, exploring with her tongue, far more curious than she ever used to be. The veins in my shaft thicken, my crown swelling as my balls draw up. If I don't do something soon, I'm going to shoot my load into her questing mouth. I tug on her hair, needing her to back off, even though I would give my left nut to watch her swallow my cum.

Instead of stopping, she shifts and licks the underside of my balls. Holy fuck. Who is *this* Olivia? While one part of me loves it, wants to see how far I can push her, there is another side of me that fights down the rising jealousy. Christ, I didn't expect her to stay celibate after me, but the vision of her with another guy shatters me completely. Truthfully, I want her to be with a good man, one who will take care of her and make her happy, but it kills me to think of someone other than me or Luca touching her. My cock jumps in her mouth.

"Enough," I say and once again she stiffens at the control in my voice, and I lecture myself. *This is Liv.* I soften my tone. "On your back."

I nudge her shoulder, and she falls back onto the bed, her hair splaying. Her arms go over her head, and I look at her wrists, wanting to tie them to the headboard. I slide up her body. My cock nestles between her legs.

As much as I hate to move, I say, "I need to get a condom."

She holds me to her. "No, like this."

"You sure Liv?"

"I'm clean, and I'm on the pill."

"I'm clean, too."

"I know," she says, and brushes my hair from my face in such a loving manner, my heart pinches. Is it possible she still loves me, even after I walked out on her? Christ knows I've never stopped loving her. She's half of my soul. But does that mean she'd accept all sides of me? Would taking full control of her frighten her or excite her?

Luca's words race through my mind. *"Maybe she'd be into all this."*

Her hands snake around my neck and pull my mouth to hers as my cock presses against her hot center. She is going to feel so fucking good.

"You want my cock in you?" I ask

"Yes."

"Tell me," I say, pushing her a little. "Tell me how much you want to be fucked."

Her eyes narrow, like she's trying to grab a memory or piece something together. "I…"

"Tell me, Olivia," I demand, as I rub the tip of my cock over her clit.

Her eyes roll. "Oooh, yes." I pull my dick away, and her body tightens. "Please."

"Please, what?"

Her hips lift, and her mouth opens and closes, like she's trying to say something but can't. For a brief moment I wonder if she's holding back on me. Maybe she is into all this. Then again, maybe that's just wishful thinking.

"I need you inside me," she whispers.

"You want my cock in that sweet pussy?" I ask, keeping the dirty talk as tame as I can.

"Yes," she cries out.

"Tell me."

"I...I want your cock inside me."

My hips jerk forward, and I enter her. As her muscles squeeze, I gather a breath, working not to thrust hard, drive my cock all the way inside her. Feeling edgy, a little out of control, I give her another inch and press my mouth to hers. Rough with demand, I shove my tongue inside and twist my fingers in her hair. Her skin is burning hot as I crush my chest to hers. Hard nipples scrape my flesh, and I move against her as I claim her body, take possession of her.

Once I'm seated inside, her sex squeezing so nicely, I tap her legs. "Put them around my back." She obliges and her hot cunt takes me in deeper. "Fuck that's good." So good I know I'm not going to last long. I pull out and slam home, and my body buzzes with need, wanting to crawl inside her and stay there forever. I power into her, and she meets and welcomes each thrust. We fall into a familiar rhythm, like we hadn't been apart for two long years.

My cock is so fucking hard and she is so goddamn hot and wet, it's all I can do to hang on. I press a kiss to her throat and pull out, only to sink back into her wet heat. Her body trembles, and she grows slicker with each stroke. I slam my pelvis against her clit, and she opens her mouth, but no sound comes. I do it again, knowing exactly what she needs. This time, she cries out my name as she comes around my cock.

"Gio," she says as her pussy clenches my shaft, and derails

my ability to think…to breathe.

Her body milks my cock, driving me toward an explosion. Pressure builds and comes to a peak, and I throw my head back, savoring the moment. Blood pulsing hot, I come high inside her, and her thighs squeeze my sides. I collapse on top of her, and her hand slides around my body, stroking gently. Fuck, I don't even have my shorts all the way off, and I stuck my finger in her ass. *Jesus Christ, what were you thinking, dude?*

A moment passes, and I inch back to see her. Tenderness rushes over me, and I feel a flash of possession as I look into her sated eyes. Jesus Christ, what the hell was I thinking? After tasting her again, there is no fucking way I'll have the strength to walk away a second time.

But how can I keep her here and keep the darker side of me hidden?

How can I not?

Chapter Six

OLIVIA

"So this is where the magic happens," I say as I step into Gio's office, just off the lobby in the main castle. I look at his desk and all the papers strewn about. He always was a bit messy, but this is complete chaos. He definitely needs someone to help organize him. I walk behind the desk and start stacking the files, putting them in order.

He follows me and presses his chest to my back. His warm breath caresses the shell of my ear when he says, "It's not the only place."

His voice, and the reminder of the magic in the bedroom last night, teases the hungry spot between my legs. You'd think I'd be sated after consummating our marriage, but no, it left me craving him again…craving more.

Someone clears their throat at the door, and my head jerks up to see Mr. Hottie, or rather, Luca, standing there, his dimples prominent as he grins at us. Visions of him and his lover come racing back and a quiver races down my spine.

Then I suddenly remember exactly who Luca is—Gio's best friend. Of course, that's why he was at the wedding ceremony. Gio used to talk about him all the time. I hadn't put two-and-two together until just now.

Feet crossed at the ankles, he's leaning against the doorframe, looking relaxed and sexy as hell. "Am I interrupting?"

"Yeah, you fucking are," Gio says, and Luca just laughs.

Bad boy written all over him, Luca pushes off the doorframe, his eyes locked on mine as he moves toward me, a slow swagger as seductive as the man himself. He gives off such a sensual vibe that my body starts humming. I've never quite reacted this way to a stranger before. It could be because I feel like I know him after listening to Gio's childhood stories—not to mention seeing him with his lover.

"So this is Olivia, the girl I've heard so much about?"

"You heard about me?" I ask, and watch him exchange a look with Gio. Something passes between them, something warm and familiar, something that makes being in their combined presence exciting…titillating.

"Of course. Nothing gets by me," Luca says and takes my hand in his. Oh my God, the man has a smile of an angel, but fucks like the devil himself. I should know. I watched him.

"I've actually heard a lot about you, too," I say, working to keep my voice steady. "Gio told me childhood stories."

He exchanges another look with Gio then says, "I'm the head vintner around here now."

"Oh, the wine guy. I guess I should get to know you better, then." I tease, feeling an instant camaraderie with him.

His grin widens. "I think so. I'm sure Gio does, too, considering we've been friends since childhood and there's not much about him that I don't know," he says.

Does Gio know his best friend has a male lover?

As his hands swallow mine, I feel a distinct connection, not to mention a flutter of nerves in my belly, probably because he's Gio's best friend and in some ways reminds me a lot of him. Both are well built, athletic, and have a commanding presence.

He presses warm lips to my hand and drags me closer. Heat sizzles through me as I become intensely aware of him. The pull is strange, considering I'm in love with Gio and have been for years.

"*Bella*," he says in Italian, even though he speaks perfect English with no accent. Since I've picked up a bit of Italian with Gio, I know he's saying I'm beautiful.

"*Grazie*," I say in return, then take in his lighter skin coloring. "I heard you were born in the states. Gio mentioned it once," I say, curious about him.

"Grew up in Oklahoma until I was five," he says, his voice a low, tortuous caress that slides through me and takes me by surprise. "I helped Gio perfect his English, and he helped me with my Italian."

"I'm from Arkansas. We were practically neighbors."

He dips his head. "Another Bible Belt baby."

I nod, and scrunch my nose "Yeah, my father is a minister."

He grimaces. "That must have been hell."

"That's one way to put it," I say, remembering all the lectures, the proper behavior I was to display at all times. God, it's no wonder I'm so screwed up when it comes to sex. I steal a glance at Gio, who is perched on the end of his desk watching us carefully, a new intensity about him that I've not seen before. I focus again on Luca, and he seems to have the same force field around him. It fans out from his body, sizzles in the air, and my nerves jump as it hits me like an electrical charge. Whoa, what the heck?

"So you're a preacher's daughter," Luca begins, and I wonder if Gio senses the strange pull between his best friend and me. "They usually turn out one of two ways." He pauses and steps closer, invading my personal space. "Good girl, or rebellious. Which one are you?" he asks openly.

Luca is clearly a no-holds-barred kind of guy, and I like that about him. Hell, I wish I could be more like that, wish I could just open my mouth and say what I'm thinking.

"I guess I must be rebellious," I say. "I did just marry Gio, and no one back home knows it. Dad would kill me if he ever found out what I was doing. Mom would likely have a heart attack, and my brother Sean, well, he'd be on the next plane, for sure."

"Rebellious is good," he says, his voice a deep, sizzling whisper, and my stomach flutters again. "And what they don't know won't hurt them," he adds, and I get the distinct impression this bad boy is talking about sex—dirty, salacious, hold-me-down-hard sex—all the things I can't seem to vocalize. "This place is pretty important to Gio," he says, shifting the conversation smoothly. "And the favor you're doing for him…well, let me just say it's damn good of you to help out like this."

It surprises me that he knows about the ruse. But then again, he's just told me he knew everything about Gio.

"It's not like I'm not getting anything out of it," I say, trying to be casual, even though I would have done it without any tit for tat. Gio needed my help, and despite our past, I'd always be there for him. "Gio is going to make a call to his uncle, and I'll be able to pad my resume helping here."

He smiles at me then turns to Gio. "Can I see you for a minute," he says, his eyes darkening as he looks at his best friend. "There is something important we need to talk about."

Gio nods and then pushes off the desk. He brushes his knuckles along mine. The contact sends heat charging through me. "I'll be right back."

"I'll be here organizing your things," I say and reach for the files to occupy my hands before I drag him to me and demand he take me on his desk.

He gives me a wink, but I notice there is a different edge to him when he's around Luca. It's subtle, and most people likely wouldn't pick up on it, but most don't know Gio the way I do. I study them for a minute. The two are close—I can feel their affection for one another—but Gio's body is a little tighter, his voice a little deeper. Does he know what Luca wants to talk about? Could it be bad news about the winery?

"We always did make a good team," Gio says before he disappears around the corner with Luca.

My heart misses a beat because he's right. We were— are—a great team. So why then, did he up and leave me all those years ago?

Pushing that from my mind, I spin around and glance out the big window, taking in the rows and rows of grapes, the staff and a few elderly guests milling about in the distance. I scan the hill, and something niggles in the back of my mind as I search for the man with the blue hat. I can only imagine what kind of man he must be to control and possess a powerful, confident, sexy guy like Luca. My cheeks flame, and a little thrill moves through me when I recall their naked display of passion. I briefly close my eyes, and my breath crashes wildly in my ears as I replay it.

"Open that pretty mouth of yours."

Oh God... As those sexy, dirty words ping around inside my brain, I press my hands to the window and work to breathe past the lust. My nipples tighten, my skin burns hot, and deep between my legs, my sex clenches. I close my eyes for another moment as the scene loops through my thoughts, playing over and over again. The room grows warmer, a noise crawls out of my throat, and it's all I can do not to slide my hands into my shorts and touch myself.

I hear a noise at the door, and I suck in a breath to get my head on right before I turn.

"Don't move," Gio says. Excitement surges through me at the command in his tone. I sip air and stand perfectly still, waiting for another order. I want to cry when it doesn't come, but the click of the lock as he sets it reverberates through me and fills me with hope. I shudder, so ready to surrender myself to him completely. If only he'd demand it of me. His scent curls around me as he comes closer, each step like a delicious tap to my clit.

My palms are still braced on the window as he closes his big hands over mine and splays my fingers. His erection presses against my ass, and I'm blindsided by lust as his burning mouth presses hungrily against my shoulder. Sharp teeth scrape roughly, and I want to moan in bliss. I have no idea what happened in the hall with Luca, or what words were spoken, but as I steal a glance over my shoulder at him and take in his dark features, I understand I'm looking at a changed man, a hard warrior—a predator—two hundred pounds of raw power that is about to claim me.

I suddenly can't breathe.

"So, what's this about you being rebellious?" he asks, his warm breath feathering over my flesh and arousing me to the point of delirium. Desperation burns through me, my need for him to take me touching places so deep it physically pains me.

Tell him.

I hear a noise outside the window. God, if anyone walked by, they'd see us, and while that excites the hell out of me, I can't think about that right now, not when Gio presses his chest to my back, slides his hand around to my front, and starts undoing my shorts. He pops the button. Rough and greedy fingers shove inside my panties. I gasp and feel like I'm having an out-of-body experience. I widen my legs to give him better access, and that action seems to do something to him.

Bent over me, arm around my waist, he says, "Look at you.

All wet and ready for me. Maybe you really are a bad girl."

"Gio," is all I can manage to say as he shoves a thick finger inside me. "Oh God."

"You like that, Liv? You like fucking my finger in front of the window, where anyone can see us?"

Who *is* this Gio? Honest to God, things between us have always been vanilla, and I've never inspired this kind of passion in him before. I have no idea what is going on, but I'm not going to question it. I want this more than I want my next breath.

"Answer me," he says. "Do you like fucking my finger in front of the window or not?"

Something moves in the vineyard, a flash amongst the vines, and I think it's Luca. Could he be searching for his lover? I can barely breathe as I think about their passion, the kind of passion Gio is currently displaying.

"Liv," he growls. "I won't ask again."

"Oh God." *Admit it! Tell him you fucking love it. Tell him your fantasies.* "Please…"

His finger stills inside me, and I nearly sob. He hesitates for a second, like he's mulling something over, and in a voice that is much deeper than it was seconds ago, he says, "I want you to fuck my finger. Show me you want this."

Holy shit. Pleasure surges inside me, and I want to pinch myself to make sure I'm not dreaming. His hot breath crashes over me, tells me I'm wide-awake, and he's waiting for me to move, do something. He wiggles his fingers lightly, encouraging me to respond, and as my brain shuts down, I rock my hips. Gio growls in response and moves along with me, grinding his hard cock against my back.

Force me to my knees. Make me do dirty things.

He shoves a second finger inside me, making me feel so gloriously full all I can do is whimper. *Harder. Deeper.* In a move that surprises us both, I press one hand against his and grind my aching clit against his palm. A flash of lust moves through me as my orgasm builds, and I'm so overcome with sensation I begin to shake, almost violently.

"Yeah, Liv," he whispers into my ear, the gruffness in his voice exciting the hell out of me. "Just like that."

Hungry for so much more, and feeling a bit bolder, I bend forward and arch my back, wanting him to touch my ass again, spank it, stroke it, push a finger inside it. Own it, already. He curses under his breath, and when the slaps don't come I sway, rubbing his cock over my ass.

A firm palm presses harder against my clit, deepening the contact. Inside my pussy, his touch grows rougher, his strokes firmer, his thrusts deeper, and the pressure sends me flying over the edge. My eyelids shut against the flood of heat, and I concentrate on the waves of pleasure crashing over me. Easing off my sensitive clit, he runs soft circles around it until I'm spasming and clenching so hard I can't breathe.

He pulls his wet fingers from my sex, and I angle my head to see him moisten his bottom lip with my liquid heat. He inhales deeply, then runs his tongue around his mouth like he's savoring the taste of me. My legs wobble. Oh God, that is so freaking hot my sex clenches again. I drag in a shuddery breath as rough hands grip my hips and tug.

"Face me."

With a hiss, I suck air into my lungs as I turn and once again I see that intensity in him—a wildness—as his eyes meet mine. He's coiled so tight he looks like he's ready to snap. I feel a tug between my legs—tight, painful…needy.

He puts his hand on my shoulder and presses down. "On your knees."

When I don't move, too shocked, too thrilled at the way he's acting, he says, "Now."

His demanding voice resonates through me, and I swallow a raspy breath. Wanting everything he's offering, I sink to the floor, my mouth inches from his crotch. He rips into his pants, and a cry catches in my throat when his cock pops free. *Make me suck you. Make me take it until I choke.* He doesn't bother taking his jeans off. Instead, he shoves them down his thighs, far enough out of the way for me to pleasure him thoroughly.

"Open your mouth."

As hunger consumes me, my brain shuts down. Acting completely on instinct, I part my lips like I've been ordered, and he grips my hair, wrapping it around his hand three times. There is a familiarity in his move, but my body is shaking so hard from excitement—my lust-saturated brain nothing but mush—that I can't quite figure it out.

I widen my mouth to accommodate his girth, and he says, "Don't move. Don't speak."

I swallow my whimper and go deathly still, afraid to do or say anything and break this moment. My pussy clenches in agony, and I'm certain I'm going to orgasm again.

"Wider," he commands.

I open my mouth as wide as it can go, and he drags me closer to his cock.

"Let me see your tongue."

I stick out my tongue, and then he grips his cock, stroking it until pre-cum pearls on his tip. I groan, and he says, "Shh."

I go quiet, and he rewards me by brushing his crown over my tongue and letting me taste his sweetness. I savor the tangy taste of him, and his fingers tighten in my hair.

"Liv," he whispers, and I can feel his restraint, hear it in his voice. I rock against him and take him into my mouth until he hits the back of my throat. Unable to help it, I choke a little, and he jerks backward, like he's hurt me.

I flick my tongue out, to let him know I'm game for anything, that I don't want him to hold back, and he growls.

Fuck my mouth.

His hips move, inching forward, but he doesn't allow me

to take him deep again. I want to cry, scream at him, take his dick deep into my throat until I can't breathe. He rocks into me, his touch on my hair softer. I suck him in, wanting to make him crazy, wanting the predator back. His cock swells in my mouth, and I can tell he's close. I work my tongue harder, wanting him to shoot his load down my throat—something he's never, ever done before.

I can feel his body straining. Before he lets go, he pulls out and then drags me to my feet. He spins me, puts my hands on the window again, and in a deep, almost threatening voice that excites me as much as it scares me, he says, "Keep your hands here."

I do as he says, and he shoves my shorts to my ankles. My heart is beating so fast, I think I might pass out. He grips my ass cheeks and widens them, and I whimper, aching for him to fill me there—everywhere.

His cock probes my sex, and in one hard thrust that practically shoves me against the window, he pushes into me. Oh God, yes. I rear back to meet him, and he growls, "Don't move." Oh Jesus, moving comes with its own excitement, but staying still, putting myself at his mercy, is like an explosion to my senses.

I pant as he rides me, pulling almost all the way out only to push in again. One arm goes around my waist, walking me backward. My hands slide down the window, my upper torso parallel to the floor, my ass wide open and exposed as he seats himself all the way inside my quivering pussy.

His fingers tangle through my hair, and his commanding touch scorches me. The excruciating pleasure travels downward, and my sex clenches in agony. I want it harder, rougher. This mild sampling of the way I want him to behave is messing with my body and brain.

He fucks me, and I squeeze my sex around his cock. He grips my hips hard enough to leave a bruise. *Like that. Just like that*. He pounds into me, and even though I'm wrung out and strung out, I orgasm again. Gio must feel it, too, because he's going at a maddening pace, with hard, blunt strokes that take me to the edge. When I orgasm again, my body tight around his cock, he growls and lets go, pulsing high inside me as he fills me with his seed. I suck it into my body, wanting every drop, wanting to taste it, swallow it, keep it in me forever.

"Liv," he whispers as he completely depletes himself. "Fuck, Liv."

When his cock stops pulsing, my hands fall from the window, and I stand until my back is pressed against this chest. His hot, damp skin against mine fills me with warmth. I take deeper breaths, and my heart shudders at the hard way he'd taken me, a beautiful taste of the way things could be between us. Love, want, and need overwhelm me, everything I feel for this man rising to the surface, and I sniff as tears threaten to fall.

Behind me, Gio goes quiet, too quiet, and nerves coil in my stomach. Tears fill my eyes and spill as he turns me around. His face softens; the hard ridges are gone as he looks at me, and my damn emotions get carried away on a roller coaster ride.

"Liv," he says, tenderness stealing over him as he cups my face, his thumb sweeping gently over my cheek to brush the tears away. "Come here." He drags me closer to his body and holds me for a long time. Face buried in my hair, he breaks the quiet and asks, "I didn't hurt you, did I?"

"No," I answer. *But I want you to. Just a little.*

He holds my shoulders, and his head inches back. Blue eyes move over my face, assessing me, and then he pulls me to him again. I sag against his hard body, never having felt such a deep level of intimacy with him before. I open my mouth and want to tell him I love him, want to tell him so many things about me and what I need, but a knock on the door has us both separating, and my voice going mute.

Chapter Seven

Gio

"It was a bad idea the last time. I'm not going to try again," I say gruffly. I met Luca at our usual rendezvous place at the foot of Abrusco—near Olivia's villa. She still has the key but hasn't stepped foot into the rental room since moving into the honeymoon suite with me two weeks ago. Soon enough, once the floors are refinished, my wife and I will move into our own cozy cottage, now that the entire resort has been signed over to me.

"You're reading her wrong," Luca says. "You're too close to the situation to see what she wants from you. I've been watching her for the last two weeks. Believe me, I know what I'm talking about."

I shade my eyes from the sun and glance up the hill. "You don't know her like I do."

"Which is why I can see things you can't."

I turn back to Luca. "That doesn't even make sense."

"You're protective of her, Gio. I get that. But that girl

wants to be forced to her knees and taken hard."

"I did that, remember, and she had tears in her eyes."

Luca puts his hand on my arm, and I want to drag him to me. I won't, because I'm married to Olivia, the woman I'm fucking crazy about and don't want to lose again. Walking away from her the first time was hell. I'm not sure I can do it again, even though in one week we're supposed to fake a breakup so she can fly back home

"Those were happy fucking tears, my friend."

"I don't know."

"You need to push her. She'll respond." Luca sticks a blade of grass in his mouth, leans against the villa, legs crossed, and adds, "I guarantee."

"She's a preacher's daughter, Luca. A nice girl."

"So fucking what? That doesn't mean shit."

"It means—"

"It means shit, Gio. I see the way she looks at you. I see the raw need in her eyes, a girl who aches to be dominated. I would know. We share that, remember?"

I grab his shirt, fist it in my hands and press my forehead to his. "What if I scare her off?"

"What if you don't? What if this is exactly what she needs from you?" He goes quiet for a long time, then adds, "From us?"

The visual of the three of us together, two halves of my souls coming together to form one, all entwined sexually, is more than I could ever hope for.

"Gio, the papers are signed, and this place is yours. You have the power to turn it into something great. All that's left is to stop pretending in this marriage. Go do what you have to do."

I'm just about to open my mouth when a sound on the deck above us reaches my ears.

Shit.

Chapter Eight

OLIVIA

Sitting in Gio's office chair in the main mansion, I spin around and glance at the vineyard. Two weeks have passed since I first stepped foot on Gio's villa, and I have to say, whichever friend sponsored my trip is going to get a big squishy hug when I return. This adventure might not have been what I wanted or expected when I first started out, but coming here, facing Gio again, was exactly what I needed.

The thought of returning to the States darkens my mood, and the smile falls from my face. I've been so caught up in Gio and putting together a marketing plan, I almost forgot that none of this was real. That in a week, I'll be on a plane back to Seattle—to a life I no longer want.

Honestly, returning home is the last thing I want to do. I like being married to Gio, pretend or not. He has a wonderful family, an amazing best friend, and I want to stay to watch him transform this place into a bustling villa.

I adjust my sundress over my thighs as my mind goes

back to the afternoon he took me in his office. Sadly, I've not seen that side of Gio since. I wish I knew what brought that on, or what I did to inspire that kind of passion, because I want nothing more than to recreate it.

If only I could open my mouth and just ask.

It does beg the question—is he holding himself back on purpose? The marriage might be a ruse, but there is nothing fake about the way he touches me. I see the protective way he looks at me, and the love in his touch fills my heart. Maybe he's too afraid of hurting the good girl. Maybe that's the real reason he left me all those years ago. If that's the case, I seriously need to set him straight, to tell him I want him to own me, possess me, to devour me like Luca's lover devoured him.

Talk to him, Olivia.

I curl my fingers, worry gnawing at me. I've never been able to open my mouth before, but if I don't say something, I'm going to end up back in Seattle, unhappy and alone. Summoning every ounce of courage I possess, I push from the plush chair and stand. I scan the hills outside, looking for the man I love. He left an hour ago, saying Luca needed to talk to him.

My search for him comes up empty, so I leave his office to find his grandfather going through papers at the front counter.

"Hey Granddad," I say, since I'm now family and he insists I call him that.

His blue eyes brighten. "Olivia, my darling. What can I do for you?"

"Have you seen Gio?"

He frowns and looks skyward like he's thinking. "His folks have gone to town for supplies. Perhaps he's gone with them. Is everything okay?"

"Yeah, just some things we need to go over," I say, which is not a lie.

The door jingles as one of the elderly couples step inside. I give them a smile and inch away as they approach the counter. As Granddad attends to them, I head upstairs to the suite Gio and I share. Since the floors were being sanded in the cottage where we're to move into together now that we're married, we decided to stay put in the honeymoon suite—although I still had a few things in the Abrusco villa. It's not like I had to clear it out, since it hadn't been rented in ages.

I search for Gio, desperate to talk to him, but when he's nowhere to be found, I decide to check the winery. I hurry to the brick building on the other side of the property and wave to a few silver-haired guests sampling wine at the outdoor bar. I check the winery, but once again, there's no Gio. Perhaps he's in his old bedroom in the main mansion.

The cannon sounds as I hurry through the lobby, giving Granddad a quick wave as I rush up the steps and stand outside his old bedroom door. "Gio," I say as I knock. I try the knob, and it twists open. "Gio, are you here?" I ask as I slowly inch the door open. My ears meet with silence, but it's what I see that nearly drops me to my knees. Air leaves my lungs in a whoosh, and my vision fades as the walls begin to close in on me.

As I stare at the blue hat, I suck in a breath, barely able to fill my oxygen-starved lungs as I rewind and replay the last two weeks over and over in my rattled brain. All the little things niggling in the back of my head, all the pieces of the puzzle, snap into place, and the truth comes to me in a blinding flash.

Gio is Luca's lover. He's the powerful man who'd sent Luca to his knees.

I stumble backward, my hands holding the wall for support.

Gio is Luca's lover.

My mind races, and I blink, willing the world around me to stop spinning so I can catch up. Gio cares about me, but he loves Luca. This has to be why he left me.

Needing answers, I hurry from the main house to the honeymoon suite, then search the vineyard high and low, but he's absolutely nowhere to be found. Needing to occupy my hands and mind until Gio shows up, I decide to gather the last of my things from Abrusco villa.

When I reach the cottage, I hurry inside and race up the steps, but voices outside stop me. My heart crashes, and I pad quietly to the patio doors. Oh God, it's Gio and Luca. Could they be...

I quietly open the door and hear, "All that's left is to stop pretending in this marriage. Go do what you have to do."

Chapter Nine

Tears burn my eyes as I overhear the two lovers discussing me, and apprehension surges inside me. It hurts so much to know that Gio has only been pretending with me, that he doesn't want me the way I want him. He probably only went at me like a predator that day in the office because he'd been with Luca moments before. It had to be him Gio was thinking about, who he really wanted to be with. It wasn't that he was afraid to hurt the "good girl" at all. I just didn't inspire that passion in him. His intensity was reserved for his lover. A tortured sound crawls out of my throat as I spin and rush down the stairs.

How could I ever have thought I could build something with Gio? He only needed me to get what he wanted, has only been using me. I have never been enough for him, have never inspired him in the bedroom the way Luca does.

Phone in hand and desperately needing to get as far away from here as possible, I continue to run. I don't care about my luggage, all I need is my passport. I can send for my things later. I rush to the main road and find in my history the number to the cab company that had dropped me off two weeks ago. The line clicks through, and I'm about to give my location when Gio's voice stops me.

"What are you doing?" he asks, his tone hard, deep. I spin to face him, and he takes my phone and shoves it in his back pocket.

"I'm leaving, Gio."

"You think I'm going to let you leave?"

"I heard you and Luca," I blurt out.

"What did you hear?" He steps closer, his scent swirling around me and making it harder and harder to think.

Instead of answering, I say, "I saw you with him, too. That first day I arrived. I saw the way you took him, commanded him. I…I didn't know it was you until just now."

He steps into me, his hard body crowding mine, overwhelming my senses.

"And?"

I play with the hem of my sundress, wringing it in my shaky hands. "You were faking it with me, to get what you wanted."

"Is that what you think?"

"It was Luca you wanted all along."

"You want to know what I was faking, Olivia," he asks in a deep voice that I barely recognize, the same hard voice he'd used with Luca that day beneath my deck.

"Yes, no…I don't know," I say as the man before me transforms, turns into the predator I desperately want to take me.

"I was pretending to be a gentleman."

I gasp as his fingers close around my wrist and tighten.

"I…I…don't…" As he gazes at me with those deep blue eyes, adrenaline buzzes through me, and I look away, unable to hold his stare.

"I left you, Olivia, because I protect what's mine."

As gravel shifts beneath my shoes, understanding dawns. "You were protecting me"—I lift my head slowly until my eyes meet his—"from you."

"I'm a goddamn animal in the bedroom, Liv. A fucking bastard sometimes, and you're a good girl. I didn't want to hurt you. Corrupt you." His thumb rubs my wrist, and the muscles in his jaw tick. "But I had you all wrong, didn't I? You want that, don't you?"

Tell him!

"Yes," I manage to say, the truth finally spilling from my lips. "Watching you with Luca was the single most erotic moment of my life."

His grip on my wrists tightens, and he tugs me to him. His eyes burn through me, and my nipples swell in response. "Time to fix that."

The command in his voice hits like a caress to my clit, and I want to sob from the pleasure coursing through me.

"Where are we going?"

Without words, he leads me to the winery, to a back door that says, Private Reserve. He locks the door behind us, and we go down the dimly lit steps into what looks like a gentleman's club. There is a bar at one side, a brown leather sofa facing it. The walls are filled with shelving units that house wine bottles. Luca is standing at the bar like he's been waiting for us.

"What is this place?" I ask.

"It's where my family keeps its private reserve. But don't worry. We have the place to ourselves today." He turns to his friend. "Luca," he says in a deep voice, and Luca looks at me, his dimples spreading as he smiles.

"Gio," he says in return.

"Come here."

Gio drops my hand, grips Luca's shirt and drags him

close. He slants his head, and his lips crash down on the other man's. I gasp, my entire body heating as I watch the passionate exchange. When Gio breaks the kiss, Luca is panting.

"Is that what you liked watching?" Gio asks me.

Since words seem to be beyond me, I nod.

Gio turns back to Luca. "On your knees," he says, his deep voice rippling through me.

Luca drops, and I stand there, shell-shocked as Gio unzips his pants and shoves them to his knees. "Swallow my cock, Luca. Show Liv how deep you take me."

I nearly bite through my tongue as I watch Luca open his throat and take in nearly every inch of Gio. With Luca's mouth fused around his cock, Gio fists Luca's hair and pumps deeper, practically burying his balls in the man's throat.

I want that.

Gio angles his head and when he catches me watching, mouth agape, he pulls his cock from Luca's mouth. "I want you both, Liv. In my life and my bed. All or nothing."

I realize he's giving me one last out, and while I've never been a part of a trio, I instantly know it's what I want.

"All," I say, and drop to my knees beside Luca. Luca captures my hand and displays those sexy dimples as he grins at me. The connection between us hits like a punch, and his heat sizzles through me.

Gio shifts to stand directly in front of me. He curls my hair around his hand and tugs until I'm looking directly at him. The position is uncomfortable, but I revel in it. His nostrils flare, and when he looks at me, and I feel his total possession of me, I want to weep with joy.

"Look at you. So innocent, just dying to be corrupted."

Oh God. This is happening. It's really happening.

His rough thumb glides over my chin, and he cups it, hard. Wanting his heat, his touch, I inch toward him, and run my hand over the long length of his cock, delighting in the solidness of his body, the way his erection jerks beneath my fingers.

"Stop," he commands.

My body ignites, and I close my eyes out of fear and anticipation. I sway slightly on my knees, my throat so dry I can't swallow. This is the moment I've spent my entire life thinking about…waiting for. Oh God, how I want to do things that are blissfully wrong, want to cross a line with these two men, be at their mercy.

"I didn't say you could touch," he growls. "On your hands and knees. Now."

I swallow a shallow rasp and assume the position, wanting the sting of his hand, the bruises his big palm will leave. "Lift her dress, Luca." Luca puts his hands on my body, shoves my dress up and lays it over my back until my underwear is exposed. "Slide them down," Gio orders.

The slip of silk wisps over my skin as Luca bares my ass to the two of them. I wait, and my clit throbs as seconds slip by, the torture almost too much for me to bear. I want to beg, plead with him to touch me, but instinctively, I know better. Gio's hand finally slides between my legs and cups my wet mound. I quiver and shift, wanting more, needing everything.

"Don't move," he says, and a whimper catches in my throat. He removes his hand, and a second later a firm palm smacks my backside. His touch scorches me, and my body grows hot, too hot. He slaps me again, and I'm almost terrified of the sensations he's arousing in me. I would have been afraid had this not been Gio. He might be a bastard in the bedroom, but I am his, and since he protects what's his, I know he'll catch me if I fall.

"That'll teach you to obey," he growls. "Now remove those damn panties and get back to your knees." I follow his orders and take my place beside Luca. When I meet Gio's glance, he drags his thumb over my bottom lip, then shoves it inside.

His dark gaze holds me captive, and I know he's going to devour me.

Yes!

"I own you," he says. "This body is mine. Anything I want, I take."

The rough edge to him excites me. "Please…" I cry out.

"Shh. Open up. I want to fuck this pretty mouth of yours."

Beside me, Luca places his hands on his thighs and shifts restlessly as he waits his turn. I widen my mouth and tip my head back to give him access to my throat. Lust consumes me as he grips his cock and slides it over my lower lip.

"Look at you," he says. "Pretending to be a good girl when all along you wanted me to shove my cock down your throat."

I whimper, unable to say much as he fills my mouth. I take him deep, taste his possession, and hold my breath as he slides into my throat.

"That's my girl," he says. "My dirty girl who likes to suck cock." He powers forward and pulls his cock out, only to shove it back inside. "I bet your sweet little pussy is dripping wet for me, aching to be filled." When he pulls out again, pre-cum drips from his crown, and he runs it over my lips, wetting my face. I want to chase it with my tongue, but don't dare make a move.

Luca is breathing heavily, and my breath is coming in ragged gasps as Gio feeds me his cock. I lick and suck and can feel blood fill his veins. He's so close, and I want so desperately to taste him.

"That's it," he said. "Suck me like the dirty girl you really are."

I suck and swirl my tongue, and he grabs my hair roughly and tugs, opening my throat even more. He rocks into me and twists his fingers in my hair. He grunts and his cock pulses as he releases in my mouth. I swallow his cum, wanting to cry out in pleasure as it pours down my throat.

When he stops throbbing, he pulls out, and I lick my lips to get every last drop. He goes quiet as he watches me, like he's checking in on my well-being.

"Luca, clear the counter." Luca stands and hurries to the bar. "I want my mouth on your pussy," Gio says, a new urgency in his voice as he shackles my wrists with his big hands and pulls me to my feet. "I going to eat you, and tongue fuck you, and make you come so fucking hard, this time next week you'll still feel my mouth on your cunt."

Oh. My. God.

His expression changes, darkens, and he gazes at me like a man possessed, like a man daring me to disobey. Face harsh, his grip tightens on my waist and, taking full charge of my body, and me, he lifts me clear from the floor and sets me on the granite countertop.

His big fingers bite into my thighs as he spreads them wide, pushing my sundress up until my sex is fully exposed. I try to breathe, to think, but can't. I can only feel. So much is happening. So many sensations rush through me. I become intently aware of the storm of pleasure building inside me as a finger slips between my legs, brushing along the folds that are slick with pleasure. He probes my entrance, and I moan as I put my hands on his shoulders, feeling his sheer strength.

His fingers tunnel inside as his mouth closes over mine. His lips are firm, his tongue rough with demand, and I can taste his need as he ravages me. He tears his mouth from mine and rips the front of my dress open. The buttons scatter to the floor, and I gasp. His grin is slow, predatory, an intoxicating mix of heat and desire as he zeroes in on my bare breasts.

"These are mine," he says, and closes his mouth around my hard nipple, greedily drawing it inside. My skin grows tight as he sucks and licks, then bites down with enough force that I feel it all the way to my sex.

"Gio," I cry out.

He eats at me, taking his fill before he abandons my breasts and, none too gently, gives me a little shove until my back is flat against the counter. Luca stands behind me, and captures my hands, pulling them over my head, until I'm completely at Gio's mercy. He lifts my legs, placing my feet on the counter, and I quiver as his tongue brushes along my inner thighs.

Two big hands slide under my backside, lifting my pussy to his mouth. The soft blade of his tongue scorches my folds, spreading them wider to give him full access to my quivering sex. Damp heat flicks over my clit, and I buck against his face, the sweet torture making me throb.

His questing tongue probes my opening, swirls, and an orgasm pulls at me. I'm trembling so hard that if Luca weren't holding me I could very well vibrate and fall off the counter. Gio's tongue sinks deep. It feels so goddamn good, I power upward, my pussy wanting every inch.

Luca groans. "Fuck, that's hot," he murmurs, and I tilt my head to see him. I want his touch. I want to feel his hands on my body.

"Touch me, Luca," I whisper, my gaze sliding over his hard body as a bone-deep want pulls at me.

Gio's mouth abruptly leaves my sex, and his gaze meets mine. His eyes grow intense. "He'll touch you when I tell him to touch you. Not before," he says, and I quake at his dominance.

Dipping his tongue back inside me, Gio licks me long and hard before burrowing deep. His burning mouth presses hungrily, branding me as his for eternity, and desire claws at me. I tremble and quake as flames flash through my body. Soft quakes begin at my core, and my eyes fall shut, but open again when a hot palm slides up my body. He shackles Luca's wrist and pulls it forward to place the man's rough fingers on my clit. I cry out, pretty sure I've just died and gone to heaven as these two men pleasure me.

Luca swirls his fingers over my hard nub as Gio dips his tongue back inside me. I lie still, perfectly still, as need builds higher and higher. Pleasure centers on where Gio is feasting on me, and when he removes his tongue and shoves two hard fingers inside me, an explosion rockets through me.

"Yes," I whimper as I erupt, my entire body shuddering so hard I can barely see straight. They stay between my legs until I ride out the waves, then Gio tugs my hands, and sits me up. I'm so dazed I just stare at him, and he looks back from those heavy-lidded eyes.

"Still with me, Liv?" he asks, his voice softer than before.

I nod, and my heart soars with the love I feel for him. He's a beast, yes, but he's checking on me, protecting me, and showing concern for my well-being. I couldn't love him any more than I do right now.

"Tell me," he says. "I need to hear it."

"I'm still with you," I say. *Always.*

Behind me, Luca is pouring something into a glass. He presses it into my hand and says, "Drink." I swallow and wet my parched throat with the bubbly wine. Gio takes the glass from me and then does the same. Then Luca has a drink. Sure I'm naked and having sex with two men, but there is something so very intimate in us sharing a drink like this.

Gio puts his hands between my legs and rubs me. "Time to fuck," he says, and once again, I'm aroused to the point of insanity. He helps me from the counter, takes off his T-shirt and lays it on the floor. He lowers me onto it, but the wood is still chilly against my back. The hot-cold contrast is beyond erotic.

Gio crawls over me and lays his tongue against my smoldering flesh, licking from my navel to my breasts. "You are the sweetest thing I've ever tasted," he says, his deep tone vibrating against my aching nipple.

I spread my legs for him, and he positions himself in between. In one hard thrust he drives into me, and as pain and pleasure hit, I slip my legs around his waist. He pounds into me, touching me in places so deep I know I'll never be the same again. I close my eyes, the sensations too much, too intense. I toss my head from side to side, and run my hands over his lean, cut body, lust practically stealing every ounce of my strength.

"Still with me, Liv?"

My body flushes hotly, and I grow slicker. "Yes," I murmur, and he resumes his thrusts, fucking me like a wild animal and letting me know he possesses me. Owns me. In no time at all, another orgasm pulls at me, and I scratch at his back as I let go. He pulls his cock out and thrusts two fingers inside me, pumping deep as I clench around him and soak his hand.

His fingers are dripping wet as he pulls out, and I nearly gasp at the hard way he's staring at me. Eyes dark, face of stone, his hands slip lower, and he probes my ass, inching one finger in, stretching me.

"This is mine, too," he says, and that's when I know what's coming next. "Luca," he bites out, and Luca drops to his knees beside me. "I want to fuck you both at the same time." I nod, even though I'm not sure how that is possible. "On your back now, Luca. Pants down."

Luca grabs protection and lube from his pocket before he kicks his pants off. He flattens himself beside us, his cock hard and ready as he strokes it and slides on a condom.

"Luca and I are clean, but only I fuck you without protection," Gio says. My heart misses a beat, and I nod as he lifts me to my feet. His mouth crashes over mine, and he strokes my nipples before positioning me over Luca's cock. That's when I realize how Gio is going to fuck us both, and a whimper of happiness lodges in my throat.

I straddle Luca, and slowly inch down, taking his cock deep inside me. Behind me, Gio goes to his knees and grips my hair. He pushes me until I'm bent forward, my mouth pressed against Luca's chest.

"This will feel cold," he murmurs, and applies the lube to my opening. I clench around his finger as he pushes the lubricant inside, coating every inch of me. My sex muscles squeeze around Luca's cock, and he groans. I arch slightly against the sliding pressure of Gio's finger as he widens me, prepares me for his girth. He works in a second finger, and I want this so much, I work extra hard to relax my body, to open completely.

"There you go," he says. "All nice and relaxed and ready to have two cocks."

I move on Luca's, lifting up and sinking back down on it, all the while Gio gets me ready. Even though I want him now, he spends more time preparing me. Want burns through me, and I don't care if it's going to hurt. In fact, I want it to hurt a little as the three of us to come together as one, right now, before I go up in a burst of flames. Frantic, I press against his fingers, rock on them, fuck them.

He growls and pulls his fingers out, and I whimper with relief, knowing he's going to give me what I want. His broad head parts me, entering just a little, and I moan against the pressure. I glance over my shoulder and see his jaw set tight. He's restraining himself, showing me he cares about my pleasure and comfort, but I'll have none of that. I rear back, wanting everything he has to offer. I gasp against the pain, and for a moment I see vulnerability in his eyes, but then they change and darken because he *knows* what I need to move from pain to pleasure.

"Does my dirty girl like having two big cocks in her?"

"Yes," I cry out, and he pushes all the way in, driving so deep oxygen leaves my lungs in a rush. His jaw clenches, his need vibrating through me. He tugs on my hair, lifting me until my back is against his chest.

"Feel that," he whispers against my ear, not a trace of softness in his voice. "You feel my cock fucking Luca's as we both fuck you."

His words thrill me, and I begin to shake as another orgasm takes hold. He slips an arm around my waist and holds me as they both drive inside, massaging each other's cocks through the thin barrier separating them.

I revel in Gio's darkness, the depth of penetration. Honest to God, I've never felt so free. So alive. Legs and bodies entwined, we explore each other feverishly, a new kind of bond taking hold.

Luca slams harder, pounding into me as his thumb brushes my clit fiercely, the friction unbearable, the pressure so sweet, I know I'm going to come like I never have before. He wraps his arms around me. When he sucks my tongue into his mouth, Gio groans. It excites me to know how much Gio likes to watch Luca and I come together.

I move and buck as the two men stretch me beyond my limit, but I want more. I want to shoot to the sky and crash land. I want to break under their touch.

Gio twists rough fingers in my hair, and my sex shudders. Desire singes me as I give myself over to a pleasure so raw and naked, it almost frightens me. The two ride me through the tremors, chasing their orgasms as I clench around them. The world outside ceases to exist as we all give and take, the intimacy between us unlike anything I've ever felt. There's no denying this is the hottest thing I've ever been a part of, the most intense experience of my life. Luca groans and his cock pulses inside me as he lets go.

"Fuck, yes," Gio says and grabs my hips to still me. As passion and possession take hold, his fingers bite into my skin and will leave their mark come morning. The idea of that thrills me. He slams home and depletes himself high inside me. I squeeze around him, and when he finally stops pulsing, I collapse on top of Luca. Gio eases his cock out and leans over me, raining kisses over my damp back and ass, his breath so hot on my skin, it burns through me.

A moment later he settles beside Luca and pulls me in between them. My heart is so full, my body so blissfully sated, I can't even put into words how beautiful this is, how I'm looking forward to staying here with these two amazing men. As we hold each other, I know I'm exactly where I need to be, and for the first time in my life, contentment settles over me. Tomorrow my body will be sore, a beautiful reminder of this night, and the many more to come. My eyes drift shut, but Gio's voice pulls me awake.

"So what do you think, Liv?" he asks, the love shining in his eyes warming my heart and soul and arousing me all over again.

"Epic," is all I can manage to get out.

He grins. "Nah, that wasn't epic." He touches his leg. "Why don't you climb on over me, and I'll show you what epic really is."

Acknowledgments

To the team behind Scorched. Thanks for all you do!

About the Author

New York Times and *USA Today* bestselling author Cathryn Fox is a wife, mom, sister, daughter, and friend. She loves dogs, sunny weather, anything chocolate (she never says no to a brownie), pizza, and red wine. Cathryn has two teenagers who keep her busy and a husband who is convinced he can turn her into a mixed-martial-arts fan. When not writing, Cathryn can be found laughing over lunch with friends, hanging out with her kids, or watching a big action flick with her husband.

Discover the Dossier series

Also by Cathryn Fox

If you love erotica, one-click these hot Scorched releases...

HOOKED

a *Viking Bastards* novel by Christina Phillips

I like my sex dirty and disposable. I'm not into commitment or chicks who want more than one night. Until *she* walks into my life. Classy, rich and so out of my league it's crazy. A week together should get her out of my system, but this good girl is so bad when we're all alone and I can't get enough of her. But there's no way a princess can live in my world and I sure as hell won't live in hers...

RUTHLESS

a *Playboys in Love* novel by Gina L. Maxwell

People call me Ruthless for a reason. Whether I'm in the court room or in the bedroom, my reputation is well-earned. I'm either working hard, working out, or working my way into some woman's panties. But none of them share my particular kink, and I walk away feeling unsatisfied. Until I met *her*.

The List
a *List* novel by Tawna Fenske

Brainy soil scientist Cassie Michaels has spent her whole life longing to be more adventurous. To make herself more interesting, Cassie invented stories about her wild sex life—stories she's expected to retell in vivid detail at a bachelorette party. Her attempt to catalog her biggest whoppers goes horribly wrong when she spills wine on her laptop and lands in Simon Traxel's computer shop with her sexy list frozen on the screen. Lucky for Cassie, Simon offers to help her out...with the computer AND by making Cassie's list of make-believe sexploits a reality!

The Devil's Submission
a *Fallen* novella by Nicola Davidson

Disinherited by his parents and estranged from his wife, Fallen pleasure club co-owner Lord Grayson 'Devil' Deveraux long ago learned to place his trust in ledgers rather than people. But his ice-cold reserve hides the scandalous truth: he's a man who craves pain with his pleasure. Lady Eliza Deveraux never knew why her whirlwind marriage collapsed. She'd tried so damned hard to quell her fiery self and be a proper, obedient wife. But when Eliza is forced to return to London and back into Grayson's intoxicating world, banked passions reignite. Can a marriage built on secrets and pretense truly get a second chance?

Made in United States
Cleveland, OH
08 May 2025

16773964R00059